'Daniel, this [barcode: CW00342072]

Annie's eyes f... remembered the ta...

'What?' He lifted ...... with the tip of his finger.

'You know what. The suggestiveness.'

'The sexual awareness?' Daniel growled. 'But I don't know how to stop it. I want you,' he whispered.

She wanted him too. Desperately. But she intended to be strong. She had something to prove to herself.

For the sake of her daughter.

Quinn Wilder is a journalism graduate who claims her training took something she loved and turned it into an 'ordinary old job'. In writing fiction, she rediscovered her passion for transforming blank stationery into a magical world she can disappear into for days at a time. Quinn likes camping, swimming in cold lakes on sizzling summer days, riding horses over open meadows, and swooping down mountains on skis. She lives in British Columbia's Okanagan Valley and finds it a peaceful setting in which to weave tales.

Recent titles by the same author:

DREAM MAN

UNTAMED MELODY

BY
QUINN WILDER

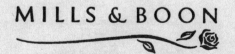

MILLS & BOON

For every mother who has ever despaired for her
'difficult' child. Take courage. Have hope. Trust love.

*MILLS & BOON and the Rose Device
are trademarks of the publisher.
Harlequin Mills & Boon Limited,
Eton House, 18-24 Paradise Road, Richmond, Surrey, TW9 1SR
This edition published by arrangement with Harlequin Enterprises B.V.*

© Quinn Wilder 1995

ISBN 0 263 79021 5

*Set in Times Roman 10 on 12 pt
01-9506-50025 C1*

Made and printed in Great Britain

CHAPTER ONE

'No,' ANNIE whispered. She stared at the destruction in disbelief. She closed her eyes against it, and then opened them again. 'Oh, no,' she said more loudly.

Ten seconds ago it had seemed like a perfect day, the early morning sunlight dancing across the immaculate surfaces of the kitchen area of Annie's coffee-shop, the mountain-fresh breeze stirring the lacy curtains at the window.

'Good morn—— Annie?'

Annie turned quickly to greet her helper, and tried to hide her distress with a bright smile. The smile wobbled.

Millicent, gray-haired and angular, crossed the kitchen and looked. Her face had been stern to begin with, but now her thin lips pulled down disapprovingly.

'Lord, love a duck!' she said with exasperation. 'How did that little she-devil get in here?'

Annie felt a swift need to defend the 'little she-devil', and the words rose in her throat and then died. What could she say in defense of Kailey after this?

She turned and looked again at the vandalism. Ten pies sat in a row on the counter-top, the crusts golden and crispy, perfectly fluted at the edges. Perfect—except for one thing.

Dead-center of each pie the crust was broken, the small, neat roosters that Annie had carved yesterday obliterated by little hand-prints that were now oozing huckleberry juice.

'Lord, love a duck,' Millicent exclaimed again. 'Look, Annie.'

With some trepidation, Annie looked. Millicent was pointing to the purple hand-prints that marched happily up and down the pristine white of the lower cupboards, forming a path right to the back door.

'I guess you didn't lock the door last night,' Millicent said.

'Lock the door?' Annie said incredulously. 'In the town of Copper?' Against my own daughter?

Millicent's stern face softened. Her love for Annie was evident in her face. In fact, there probably wasn't a soul in all of Copper who didn't love Annie.

And it was more than Annie's physical loveliness that attracted people to her, though she'd certainly been blessed abundantly in that area. Annie was tall, and full-figured without being fat. Her features were even and pleasing. If they were a touch on the ordinary side this fact was more than made up for by her astonishing hair.

Annie had hair that went down to the middle of her back, and was black and shiny as coal. It was enormously thick and naturally curly—wild, somehow, untamed and glorious. And to go with that astonishing hair she had mesmerizing eyes. Not quite blue and not quite green, but a peculiar and stunning shade of turquoise.

Annie's eyes were soft and gentle, true mirrors of her soul.

'You're a good woman,' Millicent said gruffly, clapping her employer on the shoulder. 'But that child... Where did that child come from?'

This last was muttered under her breath, as though she was doing her best to restrain herself from voicing her disapproval of the child too loudly.

'In my day,' Millicent said, her muffled comments drowned out by the tap she'd turned on, 'it seems to me we handled a child like that differently.' She turned off the tap. 'Never mind,' she said solidly. 'The pies aren't a total loss.' She looked at them dubiously. 'Maybe we can cover that part with cream.'

'Millicent,' Annie said, 'you know we can't do that.'

'Maybe we could put them on the sale table,' Millicent offered hopefully.

'The health department would shut us down.'

'Copper doesn't have a health department.'

'I know, but I just wouldn't feel good about it. You know Kailey. Her idea of washing is to let the neighbor's dog lick her hands. She could have dug in her worm-bed for an hour and caught six garter snakes before she came in here. No, I'll bring the pies home and stick them in our freezer. Kailey and I can eat them. Do you want a few?'

'I'll pass,' Millicent said hastily.

Annie looked dejectedly at the purple hand-prints that adorned her white cupboards. Short of repainting, she doubted that the stains would ever be fully removed.

'I think I'll go replace the huckleberries,' Annie decided. The town's kids generally supplied her with huckleberries, at a few dollars a pail, but she needed an excuse to be out of this kitchen and off by herself for a while.

'Go ahead, dear. I'll hold down the fort.'

'Thanks, Millicent. And, Millicent? Let me handle it with Kailey, please?'

Millicent sniffed. 'A wooden spoon on the behind is what that Kailey needs—not that it's my place to say so.'

Annie parked her fourteen-year-old Volvo on a pull-out on the nearly vertical mountain road that twisted its way into Copper. Far below her, in the valley, she could see the steep-pitched roofs of the houses in the small town. The panoramic view chased away the last of the small, dark clouds that had invaded her perfect day.

What were a few pies, after all?

She crossed the road and scrambled up a rock bluff, her pail in her hand. Then she was in the forest. It was cool and green and quiet. It smelled of the earth and evergreens. The huckleberry bushes were low to the ground, their branches weighed down with juicy, dark purple drops of fruit.

She began to fill her bucket, and the melody came to her lips spontaneously, as it almost always did when she was in the woods alone. She liked to sing, and it also let the bears know that she was here. She opened her mouth and the sound began to pour out, sweet and clear, oddly wild.

It was a song without words, an outpouring of soul, and she sang softly as she worked.

Her bucket was nearly full when a movement startled her, and she looked up. A whitetail doe stood tautly on the edge of the berry-patch, its ears flicking.

She smiled, straightened slowly, and continued to sing. She was not sure why, but occasionally her song would draw the timid deer close to her.

The doe started suddenly, swiveled its head toward the road, and then bounded away, impossibly graceful.

A moment later she heard what had startled the deer. It was the throaty roar of a big engine. She waited for it to pass, hoping she could lure the deer back into the clearing. Instead she was startled when the sound of the engine stopped abruptly, and a car door slammed.

It occurred to her that she hadn't locked her own car door. Who ever locked anything in Copper? Some unsavory type in a souped-up Mustang was probably even now helping himself to the new stereo in her car.

She moved on soft feet to the edge of the rock bluff and peered down at the pull-out on the road far below her.

There was no souped-up Mustang. The stopped car was low-slung—black, sleek and beautiful. It was not the kind of car that usually found its way to Copper.

A man was standing very still, his back to her, and not the least interested in her vehicle . . . or its new stereo. She could go back to picking berries now, but for some reason she did not.

He was looking out across the valley, much as she had been earlier. His back, beneath a black leather flight jacket, looked relaxed, as if he found peace in that view, just as she had an hour or so earlier.

The wind lifted his hair and it fanned out behind him, longer than was stylish, faintly wild.

Without warning, it happened. Her heart was beating faster, and her breath was coming in strangled gasps.

It was him. He had come back.

He would take one look at Kailey and know that he had left more here than heartbreak.

She fought the rash panic rising in her throat. She forced herself to calm down. She sank to her heels and made herself look at the leather-clad back objectively.

What had made her think it was him? The hair, of course, thick and sun-streaked brown, with faint highlights of red glowing in it. Daniel had always had long hair—too wild—and he'd said he always would.

Her heart quieted, and she struggled for objectivity. No, not Daniel at all, though the posture was reminiscent of him. The man's straight back was relaxed, but a certain male arrogance, a confidence, was relayed by his posture. But on a closer look the unknown traveller's shoulders were incredibly wide. Daniel's build had been more boyish.

She was relieved, and yet still she watched, some small kernel of doubt remaining. She hoped he would turn around, so that she could be further reassured by a glimpse at his face. That he was not Daniel.

She was getting better, she realized, congratulating herself. It had been several months since she had had this response. Sometimes it came when she briefly glimpsed a profile, sometimes when she saw a certain set to shoulders moving away from her in the summer crowds on the Nelson sidewalks. Sometimes when she caught a faint scent of a certain brand of aftershave. The thought, 'There's Daniel,' would blast through her brain, and she would feel momentarily paralyzed with shock.

Images of Daniel would skitter through her mind— his long, wild hair tangled, catching red highlights under the sun, his impossibly black eyes looking at her, smoldering with passion, his teeth flashing as his laughter danced like light through the forest.

Of course it was never Daniel, but the intensity of the response always left her shaken.

It had been six years. It was about time that response was dying in her.

Daniel was never coming back.

Thank God.

She stood up, deliberately turning away from the stranger who still stood in quiet repose, studying the landscape. She faded back into the woods. She went deeper into them, unaware of the grief that made her eyes suddenly more blue than green.

She didn't hear the car restart, but after a while she succeeded in pushing it from her mind.

The melody came again. More softly this time. And infinitely more sad.

He stood for a long time, breathing deeply of the air. What was it about air in the mountains? There was a purity to it, a crisp after-bite, that gave it a substance it didn't have anywhere else.

And, Lord knew, he'd been a lot of other places. He'd called it freedom, but he'd never been free of Copper. And he'd never been free anywhere else, he realized as he looked down at the tin roofs, silver and red, sparkling under a late August sun. From here the town looked like part of an intricate train model, nestled peacefully in a gap between the verdant green vegetation of the Selkirk Mountains that rolled on and on until they became more ragged-edged, silver and grey.

Was Annie still here?

Was one of those roofs hers?

Suddenly it seemed that he was in the company of ghosts, two half-wild kids who had roamed free through these mountains, laughing...loving. For one short summer.

He frowned. No, Annie would be gone. She had come into his life like summer lightning, and had ignited just as many wildfires. Fires went out. People moved on. Annie's mother had moved sixteen times in thirteen years, Annie had told him once. She wouldn't still be here, though she'd be twenty-four now, old enough not to be dragged around the country by her gypsy mother, any more.

If by some quirk of fate Annie was still here, she was probably long-since wed. Girls who stayed in these mountain villages married early.

He realized, suddenly and not happily, that he was afraid Annie might still be here.

The hackles on the back of his neck suddenly rose. On the breeze did he hear the faintest of melodies? Haunting? Clear? Extraordinarily beautiful?

He strained his ears and heard nothing, except the whisper of the breeze in the trees.

Almost savagely he turned from the view and got back in his car. He opened the engine right up and drove as if ghosts chased him all the way into Copper.

He slowed at the edge of the town, regarding it with rough affection.

Copper's main street, an entire block of it, had been allotted the only flat area in the town. The residential area was scattered on the steep hills on either side of that one level stretch. A one-room school, long-since closed, and a playing field, surprisingly well-tended, were at the very entrance of the town, sharing the level stretch with the businesses.

It had changed, he thought as he drove slowly down the gravel main street. A lot.

The Copper of his boyhood had been a ramshackle little town, the victim of a world in love with plastic. The small copper-mine above the town had been shut down in the fifties, and as he grew up Copper had been falling further and further into apathy.

The town had been speckled with abandoned houses, and those that remained inhabited were usually falling steadily into disrepair.

But now the town had a cheerful look. The boardwalk in front of the businesses had been repaired and painted

white. Flower-baskets hung jauntily from the corners of
colorful awnings. He could see the houses above the main
street that made neat and tidy breaks in the wilderness
that couldn't quite be tamed.

Slowly he drove by the businesses. Some of them he
remembered, though he was astounded by the res-
torative face-lifts they'd been given. The General Store.
Phil's Barber-Shop. Copper Meats. There was a gift-shop
in a store front that had been boarded up since his earli-
est memory. And a tiny art gallery where Miller's Junk
Shop had hidden behind row upon row of discarded
hubcaps. A new dentist's office and ... Annie's.

He stopped the car so abruptly that he nearly stalled
it.

It was a false-fronted building, the whitewash fresh
and clean, 'Annie's' written in red, in those bold, old-
fashioned letters that usually said 'Saloon'. Crimson
geraniums bloomed in window-boxes beneath the two
open windows on either side of the door. Lacy half-
curtains danced gracefully in a slight breeze. The outer
door was held open with an overflowing barrel of
flowers.

A sandwich-board on the boardwalk proclaimed today's special to be fresh huckleberry pie, served with
whipped cream.

He silenced the big engine of his car with a flick of
his wrist, telling himself that he'd never been able to
resist huckleberries.

He got out of the car, automatically went to lock it,
remembered that this was Copper, and dropped the keys
into his pocket.

Slowly, his heart in his throat, which was an unusually
strong reaction to huckleberries even for him, he went

up the three shallow steps to the boardwalk, crossed it, and opened the squeaky screen-door to Annie's.

A bell rang, but there was no immediate response. Annie's seemed empty.

He sat down at one of the tables, his heart still beating too swiftly, and feeling as if it were in his throat instead of in his chest. Would she have changed? Aged?

Please don't be her.

His gaze went around the room. It had to be her. The room had Annie written all over it. Fresh flowers in pretty hand-thrown pots were on every table. The tables and chairs were unmatched, a wonderful hodge-podge of old wood. Antiques, most of them, but not refinished in any way. It smelled so good in here. Like flowers and wood and baking and coffee.

An angular old woman came out of the back, and looked at him sternly.

He felt his heart plummet to the bottom of his toes. Relief, he told himself firmly. What would he and Annie have to say to each other after all these years, anyway?

'What can I get you?'

'Coffee, please. And some of that huckleberry pie. It's been years since I had huckleberry pie.'

'It might be a few more years, if you're just passing through. Our huckleberry pie met with a small disaster this morning. Sorry, I forgot to change the sign. I can get you a menu, or I can recommend the huckleberry cake.'

'Sure, that would be fine. The cake.'

That ramrod-straight back was turned to him. He didn't know the woman. Once he had known everybody in Copper. Was she Annie? It was a common enough name, after all.

Coffee, rich, dark and aromatic, was snapped in front of him a few moments later.

'The cake takes a bit to heat. We don't like microwaves.'

From the way she was looking at him, he suspected that black leather was also disapproved of.

'Here's something to look at while you wait.'

She tossed a paper down in front of him and left him on his own. He looked over the paper with interest. It was a giant ad for the town of Copper, done in an old-fashioned newspaper format. It was well-executed enough that he looked for an indication of who had produced it, and found that it had been published by the Copper Chamber of Commerce.

'What Chamber of Commerce?' he muttered to himself. In Copper?

The door creaked open behind him. It didn't open wide enough for the bell to ring, and he turned to see a small girl in faded denim overalls and a none-too-clean yellow shirt marching confidently across the floor. He guessed her to be four, or perhaps five. He wouldn't even have known she was a girl except for the mane of ebony curls that looped her cherubic face.

Without hesitation she came to his table, pulled out the other chair, and plunked herself down on it. She smoothed out a rather wrinkled piece of paper, fished a crayon out of her overalls and, without glancing at him, her pink tongue stuck out between pearly-white teeth, she began to labor over the paper.

'Hello,' he ventured.

'Not allowed to talk to strangers,' she told him, glancing up at him with censure. Her eyes were as black as her hair, sparkling with pure devilment. She returned to her work. He looked at her with consternation, shrugged, and looked back at his paper.

'What does flatulent mean?'

'I beg your pardon?' He was buying time, taken aback, not only by the unusual question but by her easy and correct pronunciation of the word.

'What does flatulent mean?' she asked him impatiently.

'I thought you weren't allowed to talk to strangers,' he hedged.

'You don't seem *that* strange.'

'Thank you,' he said drily.

'So, what does it mean?'

He could see that she was not going to be put off. In a flash of inspiration he told her that he thought she should ask her mother or her father.

'I don't have a father,' she informed him matter-of-factly. 'Would it be a good name for a cat?'

'No.'

'Oh. What's your name?' she asked, as if she might entertain that as a substitute name for her cat.

'Daniel. And yours?'

She didn't look up from her labored efforts, nor did she answer immediately. 'Simone,' she finally said.

'Well, Simone, I'm——'

The door burst open, the bells tinkling madly. 'You little devil——'

Simone slid down from her chair. 'I think I have to go now.' She tucked her crayon safely inside her bib pocket. 'This is for you,' she said gravely, folding the wrinkled paper carefully and handing it to him.

'Thank you,' he said, just as gravely.

A harried-looking young woman had taken a good strong hold on Simone's hand. 'I'm sorry,' she said distractedly to him.

The mother was very young, and very obviously pregnant again. 'How could you do that to me?' she asked the little girl. 'I've been worried sick...' Her voice faded, and the door tinkled again as they left.

Curiously, Daniel opened his piece of paper. It had four letters on it, each done in a different color. They were three inches high and quite wobbly.

POOP.

The older woman re-emerged with his cake. She shot a black look at the small figure being led past the front window.

'Disaster,' she muttered with a shake of her head.

He didn't know if she was still referring to the pies this morning or not. Surely one didn't look at a beautiful five-year-old child and proclaim her a disaster? He looked at his 'gift' from Simone. Then again...

'Are you Annie?' he asked.

'Lord, love a duck, no.'

A back door slammed. 'Millicent!'

'That'll be Annie, now.'

She came through the door that led from kitchen to the table area, a bucket in one hand, dressed casually in a white short-sleeved blouse and a wide pink cotton skirt, cinched tight at the waist with a white belt.

She was every bit as beautiful as he remembered, her hair, long and shiny, dancing in wild disarray around her face, her eyes the exact color of Copper Hot Springs, hidden up there above the ridge. She had a faint golden tan and her cheeks had a high, healthy color in them, glowing. She wore no lipstick, and yet her lips, wide and sensual, drew his eye. They were shining, as if she had just licked them.

He found himself scraping back his chair and standing. 'Annie,' he said softly.

She stared at him, and the color leached from her cheeks. In her eyes he could have sworn he saw fear.

The bucket dropped from her hands, and huckleberries went everywhere.

It was probably a good thing. If she hadn't dropped the berries, what would have stopped him from crossing the space between them, putting his hands around her waist, lifting her in the air and swinging her around, the way he'd always done when he said hello to Annie?

Six years of pain should be enough to stop a man, he told himself, regarding her more warily. He didn't like it that she still wielded some crazy power over him after all this time.

But she was different, after all. There was no warm welcome in her face, only a wariness that matched his own.

She was more womanly than she used to be, he noticed reluctantly. She used to remind him of a young filly— all energy and long legs. Now her figure had matured, fuller breasts and hips giving her that hourglass look. But his reaction to her was precisely the same—a knife-sharp feeling of desire clutched at his stomach.

It shocked him.

All these years between them, as difficult and messy to navigate as the huckleberries scattered across the floor.

'Daniel,' she finally said, regaining her composure. He had been mistaken about the fear. It had just been surprise. 'Are you just passing through?'

It was the second time this morning that assumption had been made. He could tell by Annie's voice that she was hoping beyond hope that he was not staying here in Copper for more time than it would take for him to drink his cup of coffee and eat his huckleberry cake.

Why? What had he ever done to Annie? Except love her? And been scorned for his trouble, he remembered, with a sudden surge of an anger he had thought was long-ago dealt with.

'I was left some property here,' he offered coolly. 'For some unknown reason the town wants to buy it from me.'

'You own that old house on Elk Bugle Road?' she asked with surprise.

'It was my uncle's.'

'I didn't know that.'

He had the feeling that, had she known, the town might not have made him an offer on his property. Why? And when had Annie started running the town?

'The town wants to buy it because we've been fixing up an old house every year for a few years now. We sell raffle tickets on them. It's been a good way to bring people back to Copper.'

It was a good idea. He might have appreciated it more if he hadn't been so aware of the faint strain in her voice, as if she was striving to keep it businesslike and friendly at the same time.

He didn't like it that Annie had to struggle to be friendly with him.

'As we stated in the letter to your lawyer, we'll offer you market value for it. Of course, market value in Copper isn't much.'

All the way here he'd thought about selling that old place. He'd thought about what a relief it would be to break his last tie with Copper. His childhood home had burned down. Once his uncle's place was gone there was nothing left to tie him to this place. Nothing.

So the next words out of his mouth completely astonished him. 'I've decided not to sell.'

For some reason Annie's startled intake of breath filled him with a grim satisfaction.

CHAPTER TWO

DANIEL had changed, Annie thought, looking at him distractedly. When he had left Copper six years ago he had been twenty-two. He'd been a boy.

He must be twenty-eight now, and the boy was gone from him. Daniel was a man now. Unmistakably, powerfully, irrevocably male. He had filled out. Boyish slenderness had become masculine sleekness. His legs, always long, now looked undeniably muscular where faded jeans clung to thighs. His shoulders were broader and his chest was deeper. The youthful playfulness was gone from his features. There was a look of leashed potency about him, an unsettling maturity in the lines of his face and in the depth of his eyes.

Still, a hint of devilment lingered in those pitch-black eyes, untamed. And his hair was still too long, thick and silky, brushing at the collar of a jacket that spoke subtly of success and money. She remembered the car. It also was a symbol of success and money, nothing subtle about it.

Millicent bustled by with a broom and a dustpan.

'Huckleberry hell around here this morning,' she muttered.

Daniel burst out laughing, and Annie stared at him. He threw back his head to laugh, as he always had. His teeth were straight and white and perfect. For a moment, for just a moment, he was the boy she had loved—reckless, laughter-filled, unconsciously but potently sensual.

A yearning cut through her like a knife. Nothing in the world could have scared her as much as the power of that desire.

'Annie, have a cup of coffee with me.' His voice had always been deep, husky, with a soft intimacy around the edges of it. He could say 'pass the salt' and make the spine of any woman within hearing distance tingle with awareness.

She considered the invitation. If she said no, he might guess at the wound he had left within her. If she said no, he might guess that her feelings for him were strangely unresolved.

If she said yes, she could find out what his plans were. If she said yes, she could figure out how long to keep Kailey tucked away out of sight. If she said yes, she might be able to talk him into selling his uncle's house, after all.

Suddenly it felt as if everything she had worked for was splintering before her eyes. She had worked so hard to give Kailey the kind of stability she had never had. Her world had seemed nearly perfect this morning. Even the wrecked pies were an ordinary, garden variety kind of disaster. The kind you laughed at eventually. This was not in the same category.

What Daniel was doing to her heart was in a different category of disaster all together.

The kind of disaster Annie's mother had danced with all her life.

'All right.' Her voice sounded faintly strangled in her own ears.

He turned and walked back to his seat. She watched him. He moved with that easy masculine confidence she had recognized when she had seen him this morning.

His jeans, faded to chalk-white in places, showed off the hard, faint curve of his rear end to great advantage.

Annie gulped, and turned quickly to the big glass cookie-jar on the counter when he turned to sit back down. Though she seldom yielded to her shop's many temptations, she suddenly needed her hands full. She also helped herself to an iced tea.

She went and sat across from him, aware of her stiffness.

'So,' he said, 'it's huckleberry season in Copper.'

Again, his voice stirred memories deep within her. It was a sensual voice, deep and unstrained. 'Annie,' he used to whisper in her ear, after the loving, 'Annie, I'll love you forever.'

He hadn't known what the word forever could mean to a girl like Annie, dragged from town to town, her mother flitting from man to man like a bumblebee going from blossom to blossom.

'Annie——'

She stared at him, her heart beating crazily in her throat.

'Do you remember when we used to hike to Copper Ridge and eat huckleberries until our teeth turned purple?'

She could not bear to have conversations with him that started with 'Do you remember . . .' because she remembered it all, too vividly, too hungrily, with too much bewilderment.

She only had one question to ask him.

Why did you go?

'I don't want to discuss the past,' she said sharply.

A more guarded look crept over his disgustingly handsome features. He sipped his coffee, black eyes narrowed over the rim of the cup. He lifted a big shoulder negligently.

'Okay. Let's pretend we just met today.' There was an edge of sarcasm in his voice. 'Tell me how *you* came to be running Huckleberry Hell, when you used to run like a deer, wild and free, through mountain meadows. You couldn't even cook toast, Annie. Oh, sorry.' The edge of sarcasm was back in his voice. 'I'm not supposed to know that.'

'I guess I grew up,' she said flatly. She didn't add that necessity had made her grow up. Running barefoot through meadows was not an option when you were suddenly solely responsible for a precious, small human being.

'I guess you did.'

She started at the strangely sad note in his voice.

'It's not really Huckleberry Hell,' she told him. She did not want Daniel feeling sorry for her. 'You just happened to hit us on a bad day.'

A smile teased his lips. She remembered, with a quiver that went to the bottom of her toes, what his lips had felt like on hers.

'So, it's really Huckleberry Heaven?' he teased, his tone light and easy, but his eyes still dark and watchful.

Huckleberry Heaven had been when they had eaten those huckleberries until their teeth turned purple, she thought wistfully. Huckleberry Heaven had been when he crushed her down among the berries, and looked at her with such love and longing...

'You might say that,' she said, aiming for a tone of brightness. 'I have a lot of fun with the business. I mean, it's hard work, but it's rewarding, and it's been far more successful than I envisioned when I began. We get quite a few tourists through Copper now in the summer, and, as well as the coffee-shop, I supply fresh pies and cakes to a really good restaurant in Castlegar, and to an espresso shop in Nelson.'

She was aware that she was chattering nervously, and she stopped.

Why couldn't he have gotten fat? Why couldn't he be hiding those sinful black eyes behind a pair of thick glasses?

Instead he looked better than he ever had, and he'd always looked so good.

'Are you married, Annie?'

Don't read anything into that question, she warned herself. It was the most ordinary of questions between two people who had not seen each other for a long time. Wasn't it?

'Just to Huckleberry Heaven,' she retorted lightly. 'How about you, Daniel?' She was aware of holding her breath.

'No.'

Why did she feel relieved? Was she already falling under the spell of eyes too potently sexy? She, of all people, should *know* Daniel. Know that under that easy-going charm was a soul as dark and fathomless as those obsidian eyes.

Her relief, she told herself, sternly and firmly, was because Daniel's lack of attachment just proved what she had already known. No woman could hold him for long.

She, of all people, should know what so-called love could do to a dream of stability. She'd been a witness to her mother's impassioned and pathetic addiction to the highs of 'love'. And she'd been ensnared once herself. But she was free now, and she intended to stay that way.

'Miranda Mulloney is back in Copper,' she said, her tone casual but her eyes watchful.

His brow puckered. 'Miranda Mulloney,' he said thoughtfully. 'Oh, sure, Miranda. How is she?'

If Annie had been within reach of her heavy cast-iron frying pan, she would have happily hit him over the head with it.

Well, at least his true colors were flying now.

'She survived,' Annie said succinctly.

'Survived what?' he asked, surprised.

You.

'What about your uncle's house, Daniel?' Her tone had gone cold. She wanted her information, and then she wanted to get away from him. He was too smooth. Far too dangerous for small-town girls like her. And Miranda.

'What about it?' His tone had gone as cold and wary as her own.

'Why do you want to keep it?'

'Why not?'

He obviously had no intention of making this easy for her.

'You never come here. Why hang on to something that has no value to you?'

'It's a bad habit of mine. Hanging on to things that it would be better to let go of.'

His gaze held hers, full of dark memories and darker promise, and she felt herself flushing.

Oh, sure, Romeo, she told him silently. I just bet you've stayed awake at night thinking of me for the last six years.

'Now might be an excellent time to break that bad habit,' she told him lightly, but the lightness had the thinnest vein of anger in it, warning him not to play with her heart. Not again.

'The house isn't for sale.'

'I guess you don't need money like the rest of us mere mortals.'

'Do you need money, Annie?'

She flinched away from the sudden concern in his eyes, and what appeared to be very genuine compassion in his voice.

'No!'

He smiled, a smile of such arrogant satisfaction that she would have liked to smack it off his face. 'Neither do I.'

'You've done well for yourself, then?' Somehow, she had always known he would, even though he'd been a somewhat wild youth. Daniel had always had a certainty about him, a winning way that the world would not be able to resist.

Any better than she had.

'A couple of years ago I opened a store in Vancouver. I called it Wild Melody.'

She felt a ripple of shock. Copper attracted hordes of hikers and campers and other outdoorsy types in the summer. For years now, the 'in' label on all their equipment had said 'Wild Melody'.

Still, his voice when he named his company was not full of brash pride. In fact, for a moment, she thought she glimpsed a homesick small-town boy from the mountains trying to find his way in a huge metropolis like Vancouver. She reminded herself sternly that it was really a master manipulator in Copper.

'When I started out I stocked a line of top-quality hiking equipment—tents, sleeping-bags, dehydrated foods, outdoors books.' He shook his head wryly. 'I happened to be in the right place at the right time with the right idea. Now I manufacture some of my own lines, and there are Wild Melody stores in Whistler, Calgary and Banff. Who knows what's next? Maybe Copper.'

'We don't have the kind of population here to support a store like that,' she told him hastily. 'People will come in for a piece of pie and a coffee every day, if it's good enough. But tents and knapsacks are purchases made only once every few years, and only by a small percentage of the population.'

He was laughing at her, his eyes sparkling with familiar fiendishness, and she felt foolish. Obviously he had done well enough that he didn't need her advice.

'Good Lord, Annie, you've become a business person,' he said, but not everything in his tone was mocking.

She smiled tightly at him. 'I have. Though not on the same grand scale as you, I do all right. So, if Copper is not going to be the next location of a Wild Melody store, why not sell your uncle's house?'

She watched the distant unfriendliness of her statement register on his face, and his own features grew remote.

'No.' The statement was flat and stubborn.

'Well, then, how long do you think you'll be here?' she asked baldly.

'I don't rightly know, Sheriff Calhoun. You got something against strangers in this town?'

A stranger she could have handled with aplomb.

She scraped back her chair abruptly. 'I have work to do.'

He stood up. 'It was nice seeing you again, Annie.' The words were laced with sarcasm.

He was taller than she was. There weren't a lot of men taller than she was. It hadn't intimidated her six years ago, but it intimidated her now. She thrust out her chin.

'I may stay a week,' he informed her. She felt herself physically flinch, and knew she had not succeeded in hiding it from him because he smiled with no real friendliness. 'Maybe two. I haven't had a vacation for years.'

'There's nothing to do here for two weeks,' she told him, hoping her desperation was not evident. How on earth did you hide a kid like Kailey for two weeks? She and Kailey hadn't had a vacation for a long time, either. Maybe now was the time...

'That's not what the literature says,' he said, tapping the newspaper lightly.

He was too aware of the effect he was having on her, far too aware that he had upset her, and she back-pedaled hastily.

'It was nice seeing you again, Daniel,' she lied politely. She stuck out her hand.

As soon as he touched her she knew it had been a mistake to offer him her hand. She knew she was never going to be free of Daniel, even if she took a vacation to Timbuktu. Shocked awareness of him tingled through her fingertips all the way to her toes.

She remembered how that hand had closed over hers when they walked, how those hands had tangled in her hair, how those hands had stroked her breasts and her inner thighs until she was wild with wanting Daniel.

She snatched her hand back from him. They stood staring at each other. There was shocked recognition in his eyes, too.

'Annie,' he said softly, an aching in his voice.

It could have melted her resolve like butter on a hot pan, except for the lie. The 'I'll love you forever' lie.

Her heart had been smashed by him once. It felt like a piece of china that had been all glued together. Fragile. Faulty.

She could not survive giving her heart to this man again. And there was Kailey to consider. Annie had given Kailey the gift of a different kind of childhood from her own. Kailey believed that it was safe to love with her whole heart. She trusted completely, with her whole soul.

Five was far too young to learn differently.

Especially from her own father.

'Kailey, we need to talk about what you did to Mommy's pies today.' Kailey's cheeks were rosy from her bath, and her hair curled wildly around her plump face.

Kailey beamed proudly at Annie. 'Didn't they look bee-yoo-ti-ful, Mommy? Just like the plaster hand we made to put on the wall in your bedroom, only better because the hand-print was purple.'

'Kailey, the pies were to sell to people, and I couldn't sell them once they had your hand-prints in them. They didn't belong to you, and it was wrong to touch them.'

Kailey's expression was stricken. 'Was I a bad girl?'

'Honey, you know you aren't allowed in the kitchen at the shop, but because you did a bad thing doesn't mean you are a bad girl.' Annie took a deep breath. 'You are going to have to pick me a bucket of huckleberries to help replace the pies I couldn't use.'

Kailey had an amazingly well-developed sense of commerce for a five-year-old. When she'd noticed that her mother paid the older children to pick huckleberries she had promptly placed a price-tag on her efforts as well.

'You mean for free?' she squeaked with indignation.

'That's right.'

The screech was long and ear-splitting. A little hand tangled itself furiously in Annie's hair. 'I have to get paid for my berries. I have to. If I don't, I will die. Mommy, I will die if I don't get paid. I am saving all my money for something special. You must believe me. I won't do it. I won't! I won't!'

Annie untangled the hand from her hair. Kailey was winding up now, talking rapidly, saying the same things over and over again, with a little more intensity each time.

Annie sighed and walked across the room, closing the door firmly behind her. She leaned against it, and flinched when something bounced off it. The shrieking was unearthly now, and she could hear Kailey running wildly around the room, smashing things and ripping her artwork off the walls.

Over the noise Annie heard a knock on her door. The screen squeaked open and Millicent came in.

'I was out watering my dahlias. I could hear her. You poor thing, you've had a hard day. Come sit out on the front porch. The sound will be muffled out there.'

A moment later Annie sat on her front steps, cradling her chin in her hands, trying to ignore the sounds of destruction in the house behind her.

Millicent sat beside her.

'That man who came in today was her father, wasn't he?'

Annie turned startled eyes on Millicent. 'How could you know?'

'Their eyes—and the look in yours. What are you so afraid of, love?'

'I don't know. That he'll find out, I suppose. That he'll want to have some part in her life.'

Millicent smiled wryly. 'You think he'd want any part of *that*?'

The sounds coming from the house were a cross between a Banshee wail and a Los Angeles riot.

'Was it wrong not to tell him?' Annie wondered out loud. 'I didn't even know where he was. I had heard he was working aboard a ship in exchange for passage to the Orient. I thought, even if I found him and told him, he would just think I was manipulating him into a relationship he didn't want.'

What she didn't say was that she hadn't wanted him to come back because of the baby. She had wanted him to come back because of her.

And he hadn't come back at all.

She had never stopped waiting. Not entirely. But until today she had never realized it was too late.

'Annie, I'm sure you just did your best.'

'You don't think I should tell him now, do you?' Annie asked a little wildly.

'As a matter of fact, I think you should. You've been shouldering the burden of her by yourself for too long.'

Annie snorted. 'The last thing Daniel is into is burdens.'

'He didn't look irresponsible—despite his hair, and that horrid jacket.'

Annie had to smile. 'Millicent, that jacket was worth more than a week's take from the shop.'

Millicent sniffed. 'There's no accounting for taste. Besides, if he has that kind of money to spend on a coat, he'd make a fine catch.'

'A fine catch is something you say after a day of fishing Copper Creek,' Annie reprimanded her friend lightly.

'Humph. Did you love him, child?'

Annie was silent for a long time, not trusting her voice. 'Who knows what love is?' she finally said. 'At the time, I thought I loved him, yes.'

'Then you're halfway there,' Millicent said happily.

'Loved, past tense,' Annie said fiercely. 'I won't ever fall in love again, Millie.'

'You're young to be saying something so rash.'

'No. Rash happens when you fall in love. I've seen it. It strips a person of all their power, of their ability to use their common sense. Love equals bad choices.'

'You're not your mother,' Millicent said gently.

But Annie knew there was a lot more of her mother in her than she cared to admit.

The riot inside the house stopped as abruptly as it had started.

A few seconds later Kailey padded out of the front door.

'Hi, Millie,' she said, climbing on to her mother's lap with a contented yawn. White salt-streaks ran down her cheeks, the only evidence of her temper.

'Hello, Kailey,' Millicent answered, with a mix of reluctant affection and restrained exasperation.

'Mommy, would Daniel be a good name for a cat?'

Annie stiffened. 'No.'

'Oh.'

'Why do you ask?' she probed cautiously.

'Well, *if* I got one of the kittens, I would want an extra-special good name for it.'

'I already said no to the kitten.'

Kailey shrugged as if that was of no consequence. 'You might change your mind.'

'I'm not changing my mind.' She wrapped her arms tighter around the waist of the baffling, unpredictable,

untameable child who had been born of a baffling, unpredictable, untameable love.

'Where did you hear the name Daniel?' she asked,
with studied casualness.

'There was a man in your shop today called that. He
had on an ever so shiny black coat, so I thought if the
kitten was black it might be a good name for it.'

'Did you talk to him, Kailey?' She was aware of the
strain in her voice.

'Nope.'

Annie let out the sigh of relief quietly. Daniel had seen
Kailey, and hadn't guessed. It felt as if the first hurdle
in an obstacle-course fraught with danger was behind
her.

Millicent met her eyes and shook her head. 'I'm off,'
she announced. 'Bed-time for old ladies.'

'And little girls,' Annie said, waving goodbye to
Millicent. 'Okay, Kailey, kitten, it's time for bed.'

Kailey giggled. 'Maybe Kailey would be a good name
for a kitten.' She popped up without an argument.
'Mommy?' she said as Annie tucked the covers up
around her chin.

'Hmm?'

'You know that man?'

'What about that man?'

'I did talk to him,' Kailey said guiltily.

'Did you tell him your name?' Annie was aware that
her voice sounded strangely strangled.

Once, when she had really believed he would love her
forever, she had told him she would name their little girl
Kailey. He probably wouldn't even remember, considering how shallow his feelings had turned out to be.
On the other hand, he might.

Kailey looked guilty again. 'I told him my name was Simone.'

Annie bit back a laugh that was only part amusement, and mostly relief.

'Why did you tell him that?'

'Because *I'm* not allowed to talk to strangers,' Kailey explained patiently.

Annie ran her hand through the lush thickness of her daughter's curls. 'Even if you pretend your name is Simone, you are still Kailey. And you are still not allowed to talk to strangers.'

Kailey mulled that over. 'I felt like I was *really* Simone.'

'Who is Simone?'

'A girl in a book. She never has bad behavior. And when I sat with Daniel I was just like Simone. I didn't ask him for a bite of his pie, and I didn't spill his coffee. I gave him a present. He probably wished I was his little girl.'

I sincerely hope not, Annie thought, but she continued to stroke Kailey's dark curls, hearing the confusion and uncertainty in those words.

Copper was a small town, traditional in a world that was changing. For Annie that was part of the appeal. But most of the families here were two-parent homes. Kailey did not have a father.

'I love you, Kailey,' Annie whispered. 'Just the way you are.'

The worried lines on Kailey's brow cleared.

'I love you too, Mommy. Would Simone be a good name for a kitten, if I get a girl one?'

The Copper Hotel did not seem to have been caught in the revitalization spirit that had swept over the rest of the town. Daniel's room contained an iron-frame bed, a bare lightbulb, and a dresser popped up on one side by a half-dozen or so paperback novels. The jukebox went non-stop in the bar downstairs, the steady thump of the bass vibrating the floor and the walls. It was hot, and he had opened his window to let in a horde of eagerly waiting flies.

He took to the streets of Copper, not even admitting to himself that he was wondering which one of the houses was hers. He didn't suppose the house he'd been left was habitable, but it wouldn't hurt to have a look at it.

Daniel walked the steep residential streets, feeling peace creep back over him.

Annie had stirred up turmoil he didn't know he'd had.

But Copper was always so pretty at this time of night in the late summer. The light was golden and soft. It would stay that way briefly, and then the sun would dip behind Copper Ridge and night would descend with startling swiftness.

He noticed porch-lights being turned on, people sitting in the warm circles of light, the gold of their yard-lights splashing over well-kept lawns and gardens.

What had happened to Copper?

He passed a man cutting his lawn. He liked the smell and the sound of it, but it made him ache for choices he had not made.

That ache had been growing in him for a long time. There was a craving in him for a lawn that needed mowing, and a white picket fence that needed painting.

'Sure, Starbridge,' he muttered to himself. He seemed to be a man incapable of having a relationship. He had tried, but his record was six months.

It was as if his soul was haunted by her untamed melody. He'd been grateful today, when he'd talked about his stores, that she hadn't showed an inkling that they were named after those wild songs Annie had sang in cool forests on hot summer days.

He hadn't really expected to see her, and he certainly could never have predicted his reaction to her. Longing. Longing for the way things once were. Simple and good, wild and free.

Other women had known about Annie, even though he'd never mentioned her name. Even though he had not really known about it himself until he had paused at the vista today.

'Daniel, isn't it?'

He looked up, startled. The old woman from the coffee-shop was regarding him with piercing eyes, standing behind the low rock wall that encircled her yard, a watering-can in her hands.

'Finding Copper changed, are you?'

'For the better,' Daniel agreed. He saw two small boys wrestling on the freshly mowed lawn next door to hers. Something like envy swelled up in his chest. 'I used to know everybody in Copper,' he told her apologetically. 'You didn't used to see new faces here.'

'I won one of Annie's houses,' Millicent informed him. 'Wasn't sure I'd like it here, but in a world that's too violent, and too fast, and too un-neighborly, Copper is peaceful and slow and friendly.'

'One of Annie's houses?'

'She's moved heaven and earth to make Copper what it is today. She had this fund-raising idea, back when she was first elected mayor——'

'Annie's the mayor of Copper?' he sputtered.

'Not now. She refused to run last year. We made her the president of the Chamber of Commerce instead. Anyway, when she was mayor she had this crazy idea to

fix up one of the abandoned houses that the village
owned because of unpaid taxes and to raffle it off.

'A bunch of people volunteered labor, and fixed up
an old place better than it had looked when it was first
built. I bought my ticket at a mall in Surrey. And I won,'
Millicent informed him proudly, gesturing at the tiny,
neat bungalow behind her. 'Found out later that the
raffle put twenty-five thousand dollars in the town
coffers. The publicity was incredible. People started
nosing around here looking at lots and houses because
prices were so cheap. It's a nice place to have a summer
house, even if you don't want to live here. We raffle off
a house every year, now. Ran out of ones with unpaid
taxes, though. That's why we want to buy yours.'

'It's not for sale.'

The old woman looked pleased rather than perturbed
by that. 'This is a good place to settle.'

Daniel's mind was whirling. Why was Annie giving
all of herself to Copper instead of to a man, a family,
like most women her age were doing?

A man. 'Is Jeff Turner still around?' he heard himself
asking. His voice sounded tight to him.

He had wanted to ask Annie this afternoon what had
happened between her and Jeff, but somehow he hadn't
been able to bring himself to do it. She might have
guessed how much he had cared, how much he'd been
hurt.

Besides, she had set the ground rules. She didn't want
to talk about the past.

'I've heard that name, but I can't put it to a face right
now. He doesn't live in Copper.'

'Well,' Daniel said, 'I think I'll continue my tour of
Annieville before it gets too dark.'

'Don't laugh. You could get a lot of votes in this town for that suggestion. And her a single mother, too. I've got nothing but respect for Annie Calhoun.'

It felt to Daniel as if Millicent's voice was fading away into nothing, and as if the night was closing in around him too swiftly.

Annie was a mother. Why hadn't she mentioned that when they had met today? It seemed like an astounding detail not to mention. It didn't even fit into her criteria about not talking about the past.

He felt angry. It was crazy, of course, to think that no other man would ever have felt the silk of Annie's skin next to his, but yes, he had entertained that very hope in some far reach of himself.

Some hope that Annie's life had stopped the day he had left here, that her ability to love and laugh and live had been as severely restricted as his own had been.

He felt sick with betrayal.

Perhaps he did not want to keep his uncle's house here, after all.

But then he knew the truth. He knew the reason he was here had nothing to do with his uncle's house. He'd come here to do battle with his ghosts—if he had to, if he could find them.

But, dammit, he hadn't found ghosts. What he had found was very much alive.

CHAPTER THREE

'ANNIE, I've just had an incredible offer on *Ice and Fire*. I think you'd be crazy not to take it.'

Annie cradled the phone on her shoulder and dripped glaze on to the cinnamon buns just out of the oven.

'I'm not selling it.'

'Annie, listen.'

Annie's eyes widened at the offer that had just been made on her painting.

It was ridiculous, of course. The painting wasn't worth that. Not to anyone but her. And him. The one walking around town with his blank checks.

'You begged to hang it,' Annie said, 'I told you from the start it wasn't for sale.'

'Okay. Okay. Oh—— The customer just left, with a look like thunder on his face.'

Not two minutes later, Annie heard her own front door swing open.

'Be there in a sec,' she called, knowing full well who it was. She had no intention of being there in a sec. Daniel could just cool his heels.

Daniel had never been one to cool his heels, she remembered too late, after she had left him pacing back and forth in the coffee-shop for at least ten minutes.

Suddenly he was right at her elbow, looking over her shoulder at the cinnamon-bun-drizzling. She could feel his bristling presence, smell an old familiar smell. Didn't men ever change aftershaves? He still smelled of pine and sunshine.

'This area isn't for customers,' she informed him coolly.

'Fine.' He took the icing-bag from her, squinted thoughtfully at the buns, and squirted icing on one. 'That looks better.'

She looked at the messy blob that had been deposited on the bun.

'Better?' she said, with outrage. She went to take the bag back, but he shouldered her easily aside and blobbed another bun.

'Now that I work here, could I have a few minutes of your precious time, Ms President-of-the-Chamber-of-Commerce?'

She made a grab for the icing-bag. He taunted her by holding it just out of her reach.

She folded her arms firmly over her chest. Be damned if she was going to jump all over him like a puppy. She was not going to touch him at all. It would be far too dangerous. His presence in her kitchen seemed fraught with danger.

She was already too aware of him—his scent, his height, his strength.

'What do you want?' she demanded.

He turned smugly back to the buns. 'The painting.'

She noticed the thick tangle of his black lashes. 'Well, Mr Big-Shot-from-Vancouver, you will just have to accept that there are some things your money can't buy.'

'The painting is hanging in a gallery. What is the problem?' His eyes flicked to her, ebony and unreadable.

'The problem is that it is not for sale.'

'Sentimental value?' he asked silkily.

For the first time it occurred to her how it must look— her desperate need to hang on to the painting.

It was a different kind of painting. It showed the un-
civilized beauty of Copper Hot Springs in the winter,
the steam rising off the turquoise water. At first glimpse
that was all it was. But, on a closer look, the steam held
shadows. Ghosts, maybe. Maybe of two young bodies
intertwined.

Or maybe not, as she was so fond of telling people.

But here stood the only other person on earth who
knew the steamy secrets of Copper Ridge.

'Are you blushing?' he asked softly.

'No. I am getting angry. You are making a real mess
of those cinnamon buns.'

'Nobody ever complains about too much icing. Trust
me on this one. I want the painting.'

I will never trust you again. 'You can't have everything you want.'

'I learned that a long time ago,' he said, and his eyes
trailed over her face with such naked longing that she
drew in her breath.

He had already taken her innocence. Now did he want
her soul as well?

He couldn't have it.

'How do you do it, anyway?' he asked. 'Run a
business, run the town, raffle houses, run a household,
paint in your spare time? What are you—Superwoman?'

'Yes. And if you don't quit vandalizing those buns
I'll be forced to put on my tights and heave you through
the front window.'

'Might be worth it to see your tights. Again.' He added
that last word so softly that she was almost not sure he'd
had the audacity. 'Do you still sing, too, Annie?'

'No,' she lied.

'God, I remember that——'

'I hate sentences that start with "I remember".'

'Oh, yes, Annie's allergy to the past. So why hang on to a painting that sums up the whole thing so vividly?'

'That was what it was to you, wasn't it, Daniel? A *thing*. A fling. An affair, I guess it's called. A sexual adventure. A——'

His hand was suddenly biting into her arm with hurtful urgency. 'Stop it,' he hissed. 'How dare *you* presume what it was to *me*?'

Confusion gripped her. 'Well, what was it to you?' she challenged, mesmerized by the coal-black of his eyes, the anger in them making them burn with inner fires.

His gaze became hooded, his face carefully blank. 'Nothing,' he said tersely.

Which was exactly what she had thought all along. Her eyes dropped to his lips. She knew he was going to kiss her. But hadn't she known that from the first moment she'd seen him yesterday? That this was inevitable between them?

It was not 'nothing'. Nothing would be nice and safe. They had always stirred fire in each other.

His lips dropped to hers. For a moment she was helpless in his spell. Heat, warm and drugging, so blessedly familiar, moved through her veins. Her lips welcomed him home as her heart could not.

She jerked away from him.

'That is exactly why it is so dangerous for you and I to discuss the past.' She snorted with self-derision. 'That is our past. The long and the short of it. A physical attraction that neither of us had the impulse-control to stop. And, if we had nothing else, what are we going to end up "discussing"?'

She was right, he supposed. God, it had been physical. After that first kiss, the night she had graduated from high school, there had been no going back. Just thinking about it caused an uncomfortable heat to sear through him.

'Leave it alone, Daniel. I don't want to walk down memory lane with you. I just want you to leave me alone. If it takes the painting, then take it. And I don't want your money. I just want you to leave me alone. That's the price.'

'I guess I don't want the painting that badly,' he said stiffly.

'Are you saying you won't leave me alone?'

'No, Annie. I'm saying you're right. It isn't worth pursuing. It was nothing but a couple of kids and a lot of unbridled passion, a long time ago. Keep the painting. It doesn't have much to say anyway, does it?'

He turned and spun on his heel.

Her lips still tingled. They still yearned. He could still do to her what he had always done. Her mother had been like this around men—helpless against their animal magnetism, powerless over her own passions.

And so Annie had spent her childhood following her mother's men, from town to town, province to province. When she was young she had shyly given her heart to some of her mother's companions, too. But as she grew older she guarded her heart more carefully, knowing it would not last, knowing that her beautiful mother would soon be lured by someone else, pulled endlessly by the euphoria of a new romance, but not able or willing to settle down to the realities that went into building a lasting relationship. She would not pass on that legacy to Kailey.

She lifted her hand and wiped his lingering kiss from her lips. It was not nearly so easy to wipe it from her mind.

*   *   *

The hike was calming him down. No woman had ever riled him up like that one. With a shake of his head, and a rueful smile, he remembered how he and Annie used to fight.

He'd grown up in this town; she had arrived for the last part of her senior year and moved in right next door to his parents. He'd been working then, living on his own, but still young enough to come home to do his laundry and eat some good food whenever he could. His parents hadn't approved of her mother, and had made dire predictions for the daughter.

Still, something about Annie had captivated him from the start. But his efforts to get to know her had been met with snootiness and, being a wet-behind-the-ears boy, he'd answered in kind. They'd needled each other over the fence, and when they passed each other downtown. But underneath that needling had been a growing respect—a recognition of equals, a sparring of souls.

They'd stopped fighting the day they started loving— all that energy suddenly finding another place to go.

Up here at the springs they had stopped being virgins together. He had never had anything else in his life equal to that. Or equal to the glorious months that had followed.

The months he had given himself, heart and soul, mind and body, to loving Annie.

Hell, he thought, she was right. What was the point of going over it again and again? She'd left him for another guy, following in her mother's footsteps just as his parents had predicted.

Jeff Turner was her best friend, Annie had always told him, laughing away his jealousy. He'd done his best to believe her, ignoring his mother's disapproving clucks about the type of girl who had a guy for a best friend.

She'd loved him and ditched him for someone else. It was a common enough story, except for the ending. They'd both been young. He should have recovered better. The hole she had left in his heart should have filled up, eventually.

For a long time, he'd thought his business would fill all the empty spaces in his life, the holes in his heart. For a long time it had. He'd poured himself—every ounce of his energy, his heart and soul—into building that business. But now, with Wild Melody succeeding beyond his wildest imaginings, he knew he'd fooled himself. The empty spaces, the holes in his heart, had just needed him to stop for a moment to take a breath. They were still there, bigger than ever.

He had lost his virginity to Annie. And she'd spoiled something in him. He couldn't even think of another woman in that way. It was as if he belonged to her.

And she had never released him. Scorned him. Betrayed him. Moved on with her life. But never released him.

Was that why he had come back to Copper? Was he being haunted by her wild melody and needing to be free?

He could smell the sulfur long before he came to the springs. It had been a long walk and night was falling.

And then he heard it. A shiver went up and down his spine.

The melody, drifting out in the steam.

He stepped closer to the turquoise pool that lay hidden among huge rocks.

Annie was already there, the turquoise water washing over the loveliness of her naked body. She was singing—

that wordless, aching, joyous, sad song that was all Annie's.

The song stopped as if she sensed his presence without his saying a word. Slowly she turned and looked at him, her eyes wide and vulnerable instead of guarded and faintly hostile.

It's a dream, he thought.

'Daniel.' She said it softly, almost the way she used to say it, but then a hardness entered her eyes, and her voice. 'I'll be done in a minute, and you can have it all to yourself.'

'I don't want it all to myself.' He undid the buttons of his shirt.

She sent a frantic glance over to where her clothes were neatly stacked on one of the rocks.

'Don't do this, Daniel.'

'Don't do what?' He skinned off his jeans in one easy motion.

'Let me get out first.'

'Nobody's stopping you from getting out.'

The look in her eyes could have blistered his skin, if it hadn't been so thick. He stripped off his underpants and stood at the edge of the pool, laughing at the look on her face as her eyes skittered by him to her own heap of clothes.

'Close your eyes,' she snapped.

'No.' He waded into the hot water, expecting her to bolt like a startled fawn.

He stopped as soon as the water was at his waist. She was watching him, reminding him more of a cornered cougar than a startled fawn. 'You used to like it when I looked at you.'

'That was a long time ago,' she said sharply.

'You used to like looking at me,' he reminded her softly.

She shut her eyes and shook her head, her hair, that rioting black hair, cascading all around her. She re-opened her eyes, and he could not miss the desire that had clouded them.

'I don't want to talk, Daniel.'

He stared at her, then waded slowly through the water toward her. Her eyes stayed on him this time, and he could not miss the raw hunger in her gaze.

The water was hot, and the rapidly falling night was cold. Magic. The steam was rising off the turquoise water in great thick clouds and whorls. It made the scene seem unreal.

But when he reached her and looked down at her it was real. The only thing that had been real for a long, long time.

'Is this what you want?' he asked roughly. He took her in his arms and just held her, hard and close, savoring the sensation of how she fit against him, all softness and gentle curves, her head just beneath his chin.

He wanted her with a deep and burning need that would not be denied. And he felt angry with himself for wanting her so much. Hadn't he learned his lesson last time? He knew his anger was in his kiss. It was wild and rough and demanding, hard against the petal-softness of her lips. And yet she yielded willingly beneath the harsh command of his lips.

Her skin was like warm, wet silk beneath his finger-tips, and he groaned with remembered pleasure as he gave his hand permission to know her.

For a brief, tortured moment he willed himself to stop. It was insanity to give himself to Annie again.

For a moment he pulled his lips from hers and just looked at her face, caught between his two hands. Her eyes were wide and beautiful, her skin flushed, her full lips faintly parted in invitation.

He kissed her forehead, and her cheeks, and her ears, more gently this time, and then let his mouth drop lower . . .

She had watched with terrifying hunger as Daniel had peeled off his clothes.

He was beautiful naked. Tall, strong, faintly wild. His shoulders were big and powerful, his chest deep, dusted with dark, curling hairs. His arms didn't look like the arms of a man who ran a store. They were corded with sleek muscle. His ribs were faintly visible under his skin, his belly concave and taut.

Just looking at him made her breath begin to come in strange, ragged gasps, and her heart began to beat a feral tattoo within the walls of her chest.

Her mind made a weak attempt to override her reeling senses. Her mind ordered her to dash by him, collect her clothes, and be gone before history repeated itself.

He was a leaver. Did she really want to go through all that again?

But her body remembered a different history all too well, and quivered with its remembrance. Her body longed to taste his skin and touch his hair, and kiss his lips . . . again.

When her mind tried to remind her of the price of the kind of treachery her body was all for committing it was overruled—shut off, shut down.

He pushed through the water toward her, his eyes dark and smoldering, unreadable. And then he put his arms around her, and pulled her to him with savage strength.

She could sense his anger, but it did not diminish the drugging appeal of him. She allowed herself to feel the physical connection between them.

She had been alone so long. So very long.

Now being in his arms brought some need, deliberately crushed within her, raging back to life. The warm water lapped around them; the first stars winked into the night canvas; an owl hooted.

His kiss was hard and ruthless, a taking kind of kiss. But all it took was her breath, her senses, her rational thought, her pride. Her mouth opened beneath the hardness of his.

When he pulled away from her and stared at her her whole body begged him to come back, to kiss her again, and he listened, though she spoke no words.

He kissed her forehead, her cheeks, her ears, lightly. Temptation. She tilted her lips to him, in invitation, and he accepted.

Hadn't she known, as soon as he'd kissed her at the shop this afternoon, all those hours ago, that this had to follow, as naturally as night followed day, as rainbows followed storms?

The kiss began more gently, almost tentatively, but a certain savage need would not be denied. The kiss intensified and began to glow white-hot as memory and sensation began to stoke the fuels each of them had harbored.

His lips rained fire on her. His hunger shocked her, but not as much as her own, a burning need within her let loose like a tigress too long deprived.

There was no gentleness, now, to this reunion. Passion had pushed it ruthlessly aside. Passion unleashed after being too long harnessed.

His hands on her body were possessive and knowing. He touched the hot peaks of her breasts, and she moaned with desire and longing, thrusting herself harder into his waiting hands. He had forgotten nothing about her. He bent his head and touched the fire of his tongue to her body, and it responded by twisting wildly against him.

He smiled at her with wicked knowing; he knew her intimately and he used his knowledge. He had forgotten nothing about Annie. He knew where to touch her to make her moan, and how to kiss her to make her writhe against him. He knew precisely how to make her tingle, and shiver. He touched her and teased her and taunted her. He pressed the hard contours of his body against the yielding curves of hers. He trailed fiery fingertips down to her most intimate places and was answered with explosions of heat.

For Annie nothing existed but this moment. Not tomorrow, and yesterday only dimly. In this time and this place nothing existed but her need of Daniel.

Their bodies slid across each other, growing hotter than the water. When she thought she could stand the exquisite anguish building in her no longer he lifted her out on to the flat rock, the very same rock he had lifted her on to that night so long ago.

A night with consequences he was still not fully aware of.

He took what she so willingly gave. With the stars coming out all around them and the steam cloaking them, they joined as though they had never parted.

With equal cries of release and rejoicing, they reached the moment they had both visited so often in their dreams.

When it was done she kissed him with aching sadness, ran her hands through the thick silk of his hair and laid her head on his chest. In a moment, his breathing began to come deeply and evenly.

She lifted herself on her elbow and studied him. Regret came swiftly. Sadly she traced the line of that proud cheekbone, the curve of his sensuous lower lip.

'You're not your mother,' Millicent had said, earlier this week.

But she was. She had watched her mother being ruled by her passions all her life. Watched with bafflement—not understanding it, not believing that one couldn't use one's mind to override desire.

She had watched how it ruined everything, time and time again.

She had vowed that she would never make the same mistakes.

But she had. She had six years ago, and she just had again. For a moment her feelings toward her mother swayed toward empathy.

So this was what it had been for her: a need beyond fighting.

Ruthlessly she cut off those thoughts. She had worked too hard and too long to give Kailey the stability she had never had. She wasn't throwing it away now. She wasn't.

She surveyed his sleeping body, aghast at how all that male beauty had battered away her resolve in just a few seconds.

He'd caught her off-guard this time. She knew herself better now than she had an hour ago. Even if the knowledge was somewhat terrifying, it made her better prepared to resist not only him, but also what was within herself.

With an anguished sigh, she got up from him, dried herself, and put on her clothes. She saw his pack, hesitated, and then went and pulled the sleeping-bag out of it. Attempting to be clinical, she covered him. With one last look, intended to stiffen her resolve but just re-kindling that dragon of longing that lurked within her, she disappeared into the mist.

When he awoke he was alone. He had been covered with the sleeping-bag out of his pack.

It was only then that he realized that not one word had passed between them all the time they had made love. Not even their names.

Why hadn't she called his name when that last explosion had shuddered through her? Why had she left him without even saying goodbye?

The stars winked at him and the steam rose off the pool.

He felt weakened by the way his desire for her had overruled his common sense. It was not a pleasant feeling.

What if tonight added another year or two to the penance he seemed to have been doing for the last six years?

He'd come here thinking that if he could just get her out of his mind he could move on with his life.

And instead that witch had imprinted herself on his soul more strongly than ever.

He stayed at the pool overnight, and hiked down in the morning. It was afternoon when he stopped by her shop.

The place was packed. Annie smiled at him remotely and offered him coffee.

'Don't pretend it didn't happen, Annie,' he warned her softly.

'Don't you pretend it changes anything,' she warned him, just as softly.

He got up, turned, and walked out, vowing never to return. The unfeeling witch. The slut. Why had he ever come back to this horrible place, to her bewitching Copper? And how was he ever going to get free now?

'These eggs are most... unusual,' Daniel commented to the woman who had served him breakfast.

'Microwaved them.'

'Ah. That explains it.' Breakfast at the Copper Hotel had proved that the culinary part of the operation was as immune to improvement as the accommodation was.

Daniel covered his largely uneaten breakfast with his napkin, left money to pay for it, and went out on to the street.

He took a deep breath, and his stomach growled plaintively. He could smell *good* coffee and fresh baking, and he knew exactly where that smell was coming from. A place where they disapproved of microwaves.

And talking about the past.

The one place in Copper he'd sworn off.

He looked at his watch. A vow that had lasted all of thirty-eight hours—sixteen of which he'd spent sleeping, or trying to sleep, and twenty-two of which he'd spent working like a slave laborer in his uncle's house, trying to drive Annie from his mind.

Unsuccessfully.

The anger flared in him, and then died. It was not too late to do what he should have done in the first place—what he had planned to do when he left Vancouver. He would go and say goodbye to her, give her the keys to his uncle's house, and leave this town. As if it had meant nothing to him.

Not all those years ago, and not two nights ago, either.

Purposefully he crossed the street. Throwing back his shoulders, he went in, and felt a stab of disappointment reminiscent of the one he'd felt the day he'd arrived and first walked through this door.

The woman setting flowers on tables was not Annie. She turned and smiled at him. 'Coffee's not quite ready, but have a——' She straightened and the smile faded. 'Daniel.'

If he was not mistaken there was a look of fear in her eyes.

Annie's reaction to him that first day had been somewhat similar, he remembered with a faint frown. He was a hometown boy made good returned home— not a serial killer on the run.

'Hello, Miranda,' he said, recognizing her from his high school days. 'How are you?' He was not sure that he would have recognized her if Annie had not mentioned to him that Miranda was in Copper.

He was probably mistaken about the fear. These mountain people were just naturally suspicious, unforthcoming with strangers. If he remembered right, Miranda had never liked him much anyway, though she'd overcome her dislike enough to hitch a ride with him to Vancouver the day he'd left here.

Perhaps six years away did make him a stranger. The thought made him feel oddly sad. A stranger in Copper?

She didn't answer his question. 'What are you doing here?'

'Having a piece of pie,' he said easily.

'Does Annie know you're home?'

Home. So they didn't think of him as a stranger, after all. He frowned slightly again. Miranda looked pale and nervous, as if she wanted to dart out of the door and warn Annie that he was here.

'We've bumped into each other,' he said coolly, hoping that nothing in his tone would give away what a wildly disturbing bump it had been.

'Oh. We have huckleberry pie or rhubarb this morning. And fresh cinnamon buns.'

Apparently Miranda wasn't even going to ask how he was, what he'd been doing for the past six years. He asked for the huckleberry pie, and watched her scurry for the kitchen as though she were grateful to be away from him.

When she placed pie and coffee in front of him a few minutes later, he couldn't help but notice that her hand was shaking.

'Are you all right?'

She looked at him as if he were speaking Greek. 'Yes,' she said, and scurried away again, to the refuge of the kitchen.

He looked after her and then shrugged. Hadn't Miranda always been a wee bit different now that he thought about it? She'd been nervous and prickly, remote. She'd always been a hard one to figure out.

He bit into his pie. He closed his eyes against delight so overwhelming it almost hurt.

And then the scream pierced the air. The scream of a child in trouble.

He got up so fast that his chair fell over. He ran to the door and out into the street.

'This woman is not my mother!' the hysterical voice shrilled. 'This woman is not my mother!'

He could see no one. He ran up the boardwalk to the corner and sure enough, in the shadows of the narrow side-street, he could see a woman and child struggling.

The child was in the woman's arms but fighting wildly, her back arched, her legs and arms windmilling crazily, her fists occasionally connecting with the woman's body.

'This woman is not my mother!'

The woman was Annie.

Daniel raced forward and tore the struggling child from Annie's arms. He was not certain if he was rescuing the child or Annie. He saw the child's face. It was his little friend from the other day—Simone.

Annie stood staring at him, her breath coming in ragged gasps. She pushed a wild strand of hair away from her face.

The child, without even checking who her rescuer was, buried her nose in his shoulder and sobbed brokenheartedly.

He looked at Annie. Her face was remote and cool. He suspected that his rescue was unwelcome.

'Kidnapping?' he said, raising an eyebrow at her. She looked beautiful—her cheeks flushed and her turquoise eyes luminous. He was glad he was leaving. He knew he had made exactly the right decision.

'So she would have you believe,' Annie said tersely. 'We're on our way to day-care. Could you——?'

'Certainly.'

'No-o-o-o-o.' A small wail emitted from Simone.

'If I ever catch you hitting Annie again, I'm going to tan your little hide,' Daniel informed his dark-eyed passenger. Too late he realized that the words implied he was staying. And that he cared about Annie.

The child's head flew up and she stared at him with inquisitive chagrin. The tears dried in her eyes.

'Tan my hide? What's that mean?'

'It means spank you.'

'You're not allowed to do that,' she said smugly.

Daniel smiled. 'So, sue me.' But his smile felt forced. This outrageous little leprechaun had actually convinced him she was in very real trouble. Had she been in anybody's arms but Annie's, he would have thought she *was* being kidnapped.

He slid Annie a look, hoping for an explanation, but her beautiful face was remote—a tightness around her mouth that he had never seen on Annie's lips before, and which, thank goodness, took away that soft, kissable look.

She was wearing a pair of navy-blue shorts and a pretty white summer sweater. Her beautiful wild hair had been tied back with a matching white ribbon, but a large swath of it had pulled free.

Annie stopped at a green picket gate. 'Thanks, Daniel.' She held out her arms and he transferred the unprotesting child.

'I'll wait for you,' he said.

'No. Don't.'

'It's not a problem,' he assured her.

She glared at him.

He smiled.

Something darkened in her eyes, but she didn't return his smile. She tossed her head with a proud defiance which was so beautiful that a fist of sensation closed in his stomach.

He watched as she set down the child, took her firmly by the hand, and went through the gate to the door of the neat stucco house beyond. She handed over the child to the same pregnant young woman he had seen her with originally.

What a good woman Annie was, giving that child's mother a break from her. But where was Annie's own child?

Could he ask that when Annie hadn't even told him from her own lips that she had a child? Did he want to? Wouldn't it be best just to say goodbye casually, clinically, and go?

'Thanks for the hand,' Annie said, her voice still remote, when she came back down the walk toward him.

'She seems like a handful, all right. I don't envy her mother.'

Annie gave him a strange look that he didn't understand for a few seconds.

And then a little whirlwind in pink was in between them.

'Bye, Mommy, I forgot to give you a kiss.'

'Mommy,' Daniel echoed in confusion. 'But she was screaming that you weren't——' His breath caught in his throat when Annie lifted the girl up. With the two dark heads together there could be no mistaking that Annie was Simone's mother. Why hadn't he seen that before? From the very first moment he had laid eyes on the child, why hadn't he seen?

Because of the child's eyes, he realized, when she turned them on him. She looked for all the world like a little Spanish girl, with her exotic coloring and those snapping black eyes.

'And I forgot to tell you something,' the girl told him. 'My name isn't Simone.'

Out of the corner of his eye, he sensed Annie freeze.

'What is it?' he asked.

'I'm not allowed to tell it to strangers,' she informed him, and flounced away.

He laughed, and turned to Annie. 'What's your daughter's name?'

She was silent for a long time.

'Kailey,' she finally said quietly.

Daniel felt the world tilt underneath him. Her eyes. Her age. Her name.

He knew.

CHAPTER FOUR

'WHY didn't you tell me?'

There seemed to be dark menace in the clear mountain morning, and that menace was emitting from Daniel.

He looked angry, very angry. And dangerous. His eyes, darker than onyx to begin with, had darkened to a shade beyond description. His hands were in taut fists at his sides, and the muscle of his jaw leaped in a tense ridge beneath his skin. This dark stranger was not the boy who had run with her, laughing and carefree, through mountain meadows.

But she had not known Daniel then. Not the way she thought she had. And she did not know him now.

'By the time I found out, you were gone. I heard you were en route to the Far East.' It was only with the greatest effort that she could keep the pain of that memory off her face.

He hadn't just gone. He had gone far. Far enough that she had known he wasn't coming back, that the spell she'd assumed they had both been under had been hers alone. Those had been shadowy days, swimming with pain and humiliation.

'My parents lived right next door to you.'

At that point she hadn't told her own mother. And she would go confide in his? Daniel's parents had been staunchly middle-class. Stable. Everything her own family was not. Though they had never said anything, she had always felt they were faintly disapproving of her.

'Their house burned down not long after I found out.'
That was conveniently true. 'They moved.'

Suddenly he was looming over her, his flashing eyes
too close. 'You could have found me, if you had wanted
to.'

'Yes,' she admitted, stiffly and proudly. 'I could have.'
Her words fell into a dreadful stillness.

'You didn't want to,' he said heavily, the words full
of disbelief and accusation.

'No, I didn't.' She had suspected that he would come
back from the ends of the earth to see his child. What
she didn't understand was what, in those sweetly
passionate days of summer before he had gone, had
driven him to the ends of the earth in the first place. He
hadn't been ready, maturity had told her over the years.
And if he hadn't been ready for the responsibility of
loving her, what could he have offered their child?

'Why?' His voice was anguished.

'I didn't think you had what it took to be a father,'
she said with soft brutality. Like staying-power.

'You bitch.' He said the words with such quiet hatred
that she felt as if he had struck her.

A long time ago he had left, and she had had to deal
with the fact that he didn't love her. She hadn't thought
that pain got much worse than that. But it did.

It hurt worse that he hated her, that his fury had
darkened his eyes so that she could not tell the pupil
from the iris. But pride forbade her from allowing him
to see that his feelings could affect her in any way.

'I did what I thought was best for Kailey.' And for
me.

'You thought it would be best for her if she never
knew her father?' His words were low and incredu-
lous, accusing.

'Yes.'

'How can that be the best thing for a child?' he demanded.

'Being a father is a function of biology,' she told him. 'Being a parent is something quite different.'

A dull red crept up his neck and swept into the high arches of his cheeks. She suspected that he was eyeing the milky-white of her throat because he wanted to place his hands around it and squeeze.

Perhaps she had gone too far. But she had only her own experience to go by, and it had left her guarded and wary. Annie had known her own natural father. It hadn't been much of a thrill. He'd abandoned her and her mother when she was five. She had spent her whole life craving his love and affection. Sometimes he'd actually sent her a card on her birthday. But mostly he hadn't.

A psychiatrist probably wouldn't have been at all surprised that Annie's first choice of a relationship should be with a man who would also abandon her.

But she was determined not to pass that bitter heritage on to her daughter.

'You were wrong, Annie,' he said tightly. 'I would have made a great father *and* parent. I *will* make a great father.'

'What does that mean?' she demanded, but the determined, closed set of his features filled her with trepidation.

'It means you aren't going to keep me from my child now. I have a right to know Kailey, to be her father.'

And to leave her when the novelty wears thin, when it all becomes too routine and boring, Annie thought dully. All these years she had so carefully avoided being what her mother was, had avoided relationships all together because she could not trust their permanence, because she wanted to protect Kailey.

Was all the loneliness she had so righteously suffered for naught?

Some of her anger and bitterness must have shown in her face.

'Don't try and stop me,' he warned her fiercely.

She looked at him with a fierceness of her own. But she had become a realist, and how could she stop him? She was sure he had the legal right to spend time with his child, and she was sure he wouldn't hesitate to make it a legal battle if he had to.

'I won't try and stop you,' she agreed, and her voice was frozen. 'But I will impose a condition.'

He folded his arms over his chest, as if he wanted to concede nothing to her. He cocked his head at her.

'Please don't tell her who you are. Not yet.'

'Why the hell not?'

So that when you go it doesn't completely break her heart. She knew, from experience, how worthless and unlovable a child felt when its own parent lost interest. And Kailey was not a particularly agreeable child in the first place.

Daniel had not loved her, Annie, six years ago. After the glory of what they had shared, it made her wonder if he was capable of loving anything beyond his own freedom. She did not want the answer to be written on Kailey's heart.

'I just think it would be better,' she said firmly.

'I don't think much of your judgement,' he informed her coldly. 'And give me credit for having some sense. I'll tell her when *I* feel the time is right.'

She saw in his face that she would do no better than that. She took a deep breath.

'When would you like to see her?'

'Tonight. You can invite me over for dinner.'

'I will not!'

'It seems to me that that would make it feel safer for Kailey. It won't feel as if she's being given into the care of one of those strangers she's being taught to be so suspicious of.'

There was no denying that logic. She didn't want Daniel in her house, at her table, but she had to think about what was best for Kailey. He already had, and that surprised her. She was not sure she would have expected that kind of perception from him, the man who had left so callously, without so much as a glance back.

'What's your address?' he asked, as if it was all settled.

And maybe it was. She had done everything in her power to manipulate her daughter's fate. Maybe there was a lesson in this for her. That she could not control everything, after all.

Daniel was her daughter's father, for good or for bad.

She struggled with the temptation to give him the wrong address, but recognized it as childish. Such a maneuver would only stoke the flame already burning much too hot in Daniel's eyes.

'Twenty-two Whitetail Lane,' she told him, but she was not entirely defeated. She hoped with her whole heart and soul that Kailey would be having one of her bad nights. That should be enough to send the new father scurrying back to the safety of Vancouver.

'Time?'

'We eat early—say around five-thirty. Don't expect anything special.'

He looked at her long and hard. 'Don't expect anything special?' he said softly. 'Annie, what could be more special than my first meal with my daughter?'

*   *   *

Annie had told him not to expect anything special, but her house was special. It was a small gray-shingled heritage rancher. On the semi-enclosed porch an old-fashioned swing waited for young lovers to share it.

Which was exactly the kind of thought he wanted to guard against, he reminded himself sternly.

He knocked at the door and Annie answered it. He noticed that she had changed out of her shorts into baggy blue jeans that did nothing to flatter her fine figure. He tried to suppress a little quiver of disappointment. He wasn't here to see Annie, after all.

He was, he reminded himself, furiously, killingly angry at Annie.

Or had been. Some of that anger had dissipated, and more dissipated now, when he saw how tired she looked. Haunted, somehow.

He liked feeling angry at her. When he was angry he was in control. But it was always a bitter-sweet confusion that she inevitably stirred in him.

Wordlessly she stood back from the door, inviting him in. Inside was pure Annie. Lace and hardwood, antiques and hand-made rugs. Some of her paintings, alive with colour and feeling, hung on walls covered in small-print wallpaper. It was a warm, cozy place—a home.

He felt the oddest sensation of yearning. His apartment in Vancouver was expensively and tastefully furnished. But when he opened the door there was never a feeling like this. Of homecoming.

For one insane moment, he allowed himself to pretend that he was coming home to Annie. That she would come toward him, warm welcome on her face, ready to wrap her arms around him and touch her lips to his.

He glanced at her, and his imaginative bubble burst.

Annie looked about as welcoming as a polar bear watching an expedition come across Arctic ice. If it hadn't been for his daughter, he would have been in Vancouver right now.

She led him through to the kitchen, where Kailey labored over a drawing.

Kailey was like a splash of blue against the bright yellow of the kitchen. She was wearing sky-blue overalls and a navy T-shirt edged in eyelet. She looked up at him and regarded him solemnly, and a great fist of emotion squeezed at his heart.

His daughter.

She was beautiful.

'Hello,' he said, his voice hoarse with sentiment.

'Hello,' she said, without much interest. She returned her attention to her drawing.

He sidled closer and peered over her shoulder. The drawing consisted mainly of red scribbles and blotches. 'What is that?'

She gave him a look of utter disdain. 'It's a monster. He's eating another monster. See the blood?'

'Er, yes,' he conceded. He sat down in a chair across from her. She ignored him. So did her mother, whose hair hung in a luscious black wave to the middle of her back and begged his fingers to touch it.

His eyes trailed around the kitchen. Everything was clean and cheerful. The sink was the old porcelain kind. The appliances were outdated. The table was solid wood—oak, he suspected, though he didn't know for sure. A stained-glass light fixture hung over it. The room smelled of fresh-baked bread.

He felt like an intruder.

'Kailey, go wash for supper.'

'Are you going to ignore me?' he asked her quietly, when Kailey had gone.

'Yes.'

He glared at her, but she had already turned her back to him. Wasn't that just like a woman? he thought grimly. *She* committed the unspeakable crime of keeping the existence of his own child from him, and then treated him as though he was the miscreant.

And almost succeeded in making him feel as if he was, too.

Kailey came back in.

'I meant it about not expecting anything special,' Annie said.

He stared at the bowl of macaroni and cheese that she set in front of him.

'I'll say,' he muttered. He took an unenthusiastic bite. Kailey picked up a handful, placed it on her spoon, and put it in her mouth.

'This is my favorite supper.' She fixed those impish eyes on him, apparently ready to give him her full attention now that the more important matter of her cannibalistic monsters had been looked after. 'Are you going to be my mommy's fellow?'

A piece of macaroni caught in his throat. He choked. He saw Annie's back stiffen. She was pretending to be busy at the kitchen counter. He had never felt as murderously angry with anyone as he had felt with Annie today.

Annie always inspired passionate responses, he thought. Even now, with the memory of that fury so fresh within him, his eyes kept drifting to her when she moved to the fridge or the stove, fastening on her lips, or the swell of her breasts beneath that soft white sweater.

'I'm not sure,' he said, with malice. 'What's involved in being your mommy's fellow?'

'I'm not precisely sure,' Kailey said, rattling off the 'precisely' with unnerving ease. 'Millie says Mommy needs a fellow. Are you a fellow?'

'Last time I looked,' he said drily, his eyes on the interesting stiffness in Annie's spine, then dropping to the way her jeans tried to hide her lush curves. He looked abruptly back to Kailey. 'What does your mommy's fellow have to do?'

'I'm not sure, precisely,' Kailey said. 'I don't think Mommy's ever had one before. Have you, Mommy?'

Annie looked over her shoulder, her face becomingly tinged with pink. 'Not recently,' she said tightly.

'Is that right?' Daniel said, with interest. The Annie of his memory had been breathtakingly sexy, so much so that he had never been able to chase her from his mind—other women pale and ghost-like in comparison to her, even though it was Annie who should have been the ghost.

He would have thought Annie would have 'fellows' all over the place.

'That's precisely right.' Kailey answered his question. 'I think a fellow is supposed to come calling. That's what Millie said. That Mommy needed a fellow to come calling.' Her brows screwed up and her spoon tipped macaroni on to the floor. 'Do you know what that means?'

'Not *precisely*,' he said, and was rewarded with a big grin.

'I like that word so much,' she confided in him, leaning over and putting an elbow in her supper. 'Do you think it would be a good name for a kitten?'

'Precisely.' He mulled it over. 'I think it would be a very original name for a kitten.'

Kailey beamed at him. Annie slammed a salad down in front of him, and placed a basket of home-made buns in the center of the table. Despite the fact that he was doing his level best to retain his animosity like a shield between himself and her, he gave her a look of guarded gratitude and casually pushed his macaroni out of the way.

Annie sat down. She looked regal and remote. She took a dainty bite of her salad.

'Mommy, what does that mean? A fellow to come calling?'

'It means Millicent should mind her own business. Drink your milk.'

'It must have something to do with smooching, do you think?' Kailey asked him confidentially.

'Possibly it has something to do with kissing,' he agreed. Annie was studying her salad as though the secrets of the universe were hidden among the green leaves. Roses blushed prettily on her cheeks. He found himself enjoying Annie's discomfort immensely.

'My mommy doesn't like that.'

'Kailey!'

Kailey ignored her mother and smiled charmingly at him. 'She always turn it off when people are smooching on TV.'

'Is that so?' Daniel asked, watching Annie's face with puzzled interest. Annie was the most hot-blooded woman he'd ever met. Her heat, remembered, had been keeping him restless for six years now.

She didn't like watching kissing on TV? That seemed very odd. He lifted an eyebrow at her.

She tilted her nose upward.

'So, are you my mommy's fellow?' Kailey asked, with innocent persistence.

'No. But I was, a long time ago.'

Kailey's eyes widened. 'You were?'

Annie got up abruptly, crossed the kitchen, and scraped her uneaten salad into the garbage. She started to run water into the sink.

'Yes, I was.'

'Then you do know what a fellow does!' Kailey crowed.

'I suppose I do,' he said with a smile.

'What? Smooching?' Her eyes widened as realization struck her. 'Have you smooched with my mommy?'

'As a matter of fact, I have.' He was relishing tormenting Annie.

'Kailey, that is quite enough talk about fellows,' Annie said, glaring at him. 'Daniel,' she said tightly, 'you should know better.'

'Me? *I* never turn that part off when it comes on television.'

She gave him a look of long suffering before she turned back to the dishes. He was glad she was suffering. She had earned it.

'Why won't you be her fellow again?' Kailey asked.

'I think your mom was right,' he said, giving Annie a break she didn't deserve. 'I think that's enough talk about fellows for tonight.'

'Did you like it when you smooched her?'

'I said that was enough.'

'Smooch, smooch, smooch,' Kailey cried, making kissing noises.

He shot Annie a look. She was glancing over her shoulder at them. It was her turn to enjoy *his* discomfort, he saw.

'Kailey, no more talk about fellows. Or smooching,'
he said sternly.

She stuck out her tongue at him. She crossed her eyes.
She made loud kissing noises. 'Smooch, smooch,
smooch,' she yelled.

He did not know very much about children. He *did*
know that he didn't like being challenged by one. And
that he didn't know what to do about it.

'Smooching has "moo" in it,' Kailey informed him.
'Smmmmooooooching.'

He shot Annie a look. She smiled sweetly at him, took
the garbage from under the sink, and went out of the
back screen-door.

He stared at Kailey. He was starting to sweat. She made
a loud kissing noise. She stood up on her chair, closed
her eyes, and placed one hand dramatically on her breast.

'Smmmooooooching,' she sang feelingly.

'Stop it,' he growled.

One eye clicked open. She regarded him gaugingly.

He froze his face into what he hoped was a stern, no-
nonsense expression.

'Smmmooo——'

'Sit down,' he ordered sharply.

She stood for a moment longer, then gave him a sunny
smile, sank back into her seat, and took a bite of
macaroni.

He was aware of feeling faintly wrung-out by the en-
counter. The door squeaked open. He shot Annie a re-
sentful look. She looked serene as a plaster of Paris
madonna.

Kailey had decided to talk, and she didn't stop. Her
voice went on and on and on. He wanted to hang on
every word his precious daughter said, but he could feel
his eyes glazing over.

Once he caught Annie looking at him with a faintly smug look on her face. So, you want to be a daddy? it said.

They had huckleberry pie with fingerprints in the crust for dessert.

He was thinking of a way to exit gracefully when Annie came and put a board-game on the table.

'Are we going to play Sweetie Land, Mommy?' Kailey crowed with delight.

'Daniel might want to play it with you before you go to bed,' Annie suggested innocently.

He looked at her suspiciously. Why did she look just like a cat that had swallowed a canary?

He soon found out. Sweetie Land was as tedious as Kailey was tyrannical. When he won, she told him that she hoped a crocodile would eat his legs.

Annie seemed to have disappeared. He suspected that she was determined to let him deal with *his* daughter himself.

'Bedtime,' Annie finally sang.

Daniel nearly collapsed with relief.

'Would you read me my bedtime story?' Kailey asked. She tucked a small hand in his, and looked at him beseechingly.

It was easy to forget that she had just wished his legs were crocodile feed.

'Sure, if it's okay with your Mom.'

She ran out of the room. The silence left in her wake seemed blessed and golden. He gave in to the temptation to lay his head on the table. He felt utterly exhausted.

'In here,' Kailey called.

He followed her voice. She was in the living-room, nestled on the couch. She was wearing a long red and

white flannelette nightie. Her wild hair had been scooped
back with a ribbon.

She looked like an angel. She beamed at him, and
patted the couch beside her.

When he sat down, she handed him a book.

'*Good Families Don't* by Robert Munsch,' he read.

Kailey sighed happily and snuggled close into his side.
She smelled sweet and child-like, and her warmth beside
him filled him with tenderness.

'This is my absolute favorite book in the whole wide
world.'

'Really? What's it about?'

'Farts,' the angel informed him contentedly.

'I like your fellow a lot, Mommy,' Kailey told Annie
drowsily as Annie tucked her under her covers and
planted a kiss on her pink round cheek.

'He's not my fellow, sweetheart.' In the back of her
mind she listened for the slap of the front-door screen,
indicating that Daniel had let himself out. It didn't come.
Maybe Daniel had closed it quietly.

'Will he come back and see us again?'

'I think so.' Unfortunately. It had been much harder
than she had thought it would be, having that big, masculine presence in her house.

It had hurt more than she had thought anything could
hurt to see him with her daughter.

Their daughter.

It was the way it should have been. A mommy and a
daddy, and quiet nights together, playing and laughing
and being a family.

It was a dream she had left behind her a long time
ago. A dream Daniel had stolen from her. She hated him

for coming back here and giving her the illusion of the dream with no reality behind it.

But, if it were real, now that the child was in bed she would go to him and take him in her arms, taste his lips, laugh into his eyes, playfully tempt him.

Her mother in her, she thought with distaste. Controlled by her passionate nature. She would not be her mother. She would not give in to the need that sang hauntingly within her.

She tiptoed from Kailey's room and closed the bedroom door. She paused. The house was dark and silent.

Daniel was gone.

Thank goodness.

She gathered up some book-work from a shelf in the kitchen and went and turned on the light over her rolltop desk in the living-room.

She started at a sound, whirled, and stared at the figure on her sofa.

Her heart stopped beating so fast, and she couldn't help but smile. Daniel was stretched out on her couch, fast asleep.

She moved closer and gave in to the temptation just to look at him. To drink in the sweep of his lashes, the proud line of his cheekbone, the sensuous curve of his bottom lip. His shoulders were wide underneath a casual brown open-neck sweater, and his legs looked long and strong in new denims.

She inched closer. She could hear his breath coming at deep, regular intervals. She could smell that aroma that was Daniel. Clean, outdoorsy, male.

His hair was falling forward into his eyes, and she hesitated and then reached out and pushed it back with her fingertips.

'Oh!'

A strong hand enveloped her wrist and she found herself sitting on Daniel's chest, looking into eyes that leapt with devilment.

'Let me up,' she demanded.

His other arm wrapped around her. The more she struggled, the more she seemed to get entangled in his limbs.

'Daniel!'

'You started it,' he told her evenly.

'I did no such thing.'

'Stroking my hair while I was sleeping.'

'I doubt you really were sleeping, you conniver. And my only intention was to wake you up and send you home.'

'Was it, Annie?' His lips trailed across the palm of her hand. His eyes remained fastened on her face, but the laughter was gone from them.

'This morning I was a bitch,' she reminded him. 'Now you want to kiss and cuddle?'

'I know why you don't like watching kissing on TV,' he taunted her.

She stiffened.

'It makes you want something you don't have, doesn't it, Annie?'

His voice was a purr of pure insolence.

'I have everything I could possibly want,' she informed him tersely. She tried again to free herself from him, but he was so strong.

His strength could melt every bit of her resolve. And the glitter in his eyes said that he knew it.

'I can't believe you don't have a fellow, Annie. A woman of your appetites.'

'You know nothing of my appetites,' she hissed at him with fury. 'Some men are completely controlled by their hormones.'

'So are some women,' he told her softly. 'I have a long memory, Annie.'

'So do I!' she spat, and finally managed to jerk away from him. She leapt up and stood several feet away from him, aware of the ache of that unsatisfied appetite within her, aware of the look in his eyes fueling her almost breathless hunger.

She couldn't let him see that. She couldn't let him see how right he was. 'I can't believe you don't have a gal, Daniel,' she snapped. 'A man of your charm and sophistication.'

He sat up on the couch and ran a hand through the tangled red-brown silk of his hair. He smiled lazily at her. But was there also faint accusation in that smile?

'I never seem to be able to stay in a relationship for very long,' he told her.

Tonight she supposed there had been a bit of a dreamer left in her. He had looked right sitting at her table, reading to Kailey, sleeping on her couch.

How could she still be so naïve where this man was concerned?

He'd left her. And, by his own admission, he'd left any others he'd been with.

He was the leaving kind.

Her mother had been the leaving kind. She loved with white-hot intensity...for a while. Now and then her mother had picked a man who left her first but, regardless, they were all the same, her mother's men. Charming. Handsome. Faintly untamed. And so sexy that they set a woman's teeth on edge.

The leaving kind. Annie had seen enough of them to recognize one sitting on her own couch.

'I want you to go now.'

Daniel stood up and stretched casually. Sure enough, it set her teeth on edge.

'Why don't the three of us go on a picnic on Sunday?'

She gaped at him. From her appetites to picnics in the blinding blink of an eye. She was not going to let Daniel Starbridge knock her off-balance again, not when she was still paying the price for the last time he'd swept her off her feet.

She folded her arms over her chest. 'A picnic?'

'We could pack sandwiches and pick huckleberries. What do you say?'

You're crazy, popped into her head, but what popped out was a simple, self-preserving 'no'.

'I don't think Kailey is ready for an outing with me alone yet,' he said thoughtfully. 'So should I just come over here on Sunday?'

Kailey, she remembered grimly. The bond with him that she would always share, that she would never be able to break.

A picnic would probably be safer than having him back here, in a house that seemed too small to contain him properly, that he seemed to fill right up until there was no escaping from him.

'I'll think about a picnic,' she said tersely.

'You do that,' he said with a smile. 'I'm working on my uncle's house, so you can just drop over and let me know.'

'What are you working on your uncle's house for?' she asked suspiciously.

'Somebody told me Copper would be a good place to settle,' he informed her evenly, his eyes mocking on her face. He gave her a slight mock-bow. 'Goodnight, Annie.'

CHAPTER FIVE

ANNIE paused outside the gate to the yard and looked wistfully at the tall, narrow brown and white house. It had been empty less than a year, and it would have needed relatively little work to make it suitable for the raffle.

The sound of energetic pounding came from within, and Annie scowled at the noise, then took a deep breath and pushed open the gate.

Her hair was pulled back severely, and she was wearing a very high-necked ivory blouse and a no-nonsense, calf-length plaid skirt. She had been pleased, when she had studied her reflection this morning, at the effect. She looked very prim and proper, like a turn-of-the-century school teacher. Hardly a figure to inspire passion—or one that anyone would guess was hiding quite a bit of passion of her own.

She went up the four steps to the small covered porch and rapped sharply on the door.

In some far corner of the house the pounding of the hammer stopped, and she could hear Daniel coming, her heart beating faster as his footsteps echoed closer. The door swung open.

Her breath caught in her throat. She had not seen Daniel for several days. He was wearing a sweatshirt with no sleeves, and his arms were glistening with perspiration. His biceps looked powerful and steel-hard. His jeans were old, and snug in all the wrong places. Plasterdust speckled his hair, giving her a preview of what he might look like in thirty or forty years.

Gorgeous.

'My, my,' he said, holding open the screen-door for her. 'Miss Annie Calhoun comes a-calling.'

She glared at him, feeling as if he had seen through her too-proper garb immediately. She suddenly felt ridiculously overdressed. The outfit had failed miserably in achieving its goal, anyway.

Daniel's eyes were hot and stripping as he regarded her thoughtfully.

'I'll stay outside, thanks.'

'Forget your chaperon, Miss Calhoun?' He said it with mockery, as if she was so hot-blooded that she couldn't trust herself alone in a gentleman's house without a guardian.

He was exactly right, of course. She couldn't trust herself. But she refused to give him the satisfaction of being right.

She should have insisted on staying out on the porch, in full view of the whole neighborhood and safe in the protection of broad daylight, but she stepped by him into the house, mostly because it felt as if he had dared her, but partly because she was curious about what he was doing to the house she had wanted so badly for the town of Copper.

Her mouth fell open. 'Daniel!'

'What?'

'For heaven's sake, why not just sell it to us if you were going to demolish it?'

'I'm not demolishing it,' he said with amusement. 'I'm renovating.'

She looked at the mountains of debris, broken plaster and smashed walls, and shook her head. 'Do you know what you're doing?'

'Not really,' he admitted easily. 'But it was too dark, and the rooms were too small and narrow.'

It occurred to her, and the thought was followed by an unmistakable wave of panic, that he really *was* staying.

'Who's looking after your business while you play at the renovation game?' She hoped some miracle would occur, that she would remind him of his forgotten duties elsewhere and he would lay down his hammer and head back to Vancouver.

He just smiled that easy, totally aggravating smile. 'I haven't had a vacation for a long time. There's nothing about the business that I can't do from here, for the time being.'

She took those four words—for the time being—and cradled them in her heart. 'This doesn't look like much of a vacation.'

'I'm enjoying it.'

She looked at him. He did, indeed, look as if he was enjoying himself—his stance relaxed, his face alive, those dark eyes twinkling with unmistakable...challenge.

It had been a mistake to come in here.

'Do you want a tour?'

'No.' But she was warring with her own curiosity and it must have showed.

'Come on, Annie. You love these old places. I remember I couldn't keep you out of old houses, you were always wandering through those abandoned places with a dreamy look on your face.'

'Was I?' she said coolly. But in truth she remembered very well. The solid old houses had seemed to represent a piece of history, when things were gentler and slower. They represented a day of strong family values and traditions. Days when people sat on their front porches and called to friends, when the children played croquet in the yard on Sunday. When a man and a woman said 'I do' and meant it for the rest of their days. To a girl who had been raised in a transient life-style, the ghosts that had inhabited those houses had whispered to her of permanence.

She was embarrassed to find that such fairytales still held a fond place in her heart.

He took her arm and escorted her past a shell of a wall. She didn't resist.

'I'm taking out the hallway,' he explained to her, 'to make the living-room larger and brighter. And then I'm knocking out the wall between the two downstairs bedrooms to make one large one.'

'Your whole house is going to collapse around your ears,' she predicted dourly. She could visualize the changes he was going to make, and knew they would be wonderful.

'I left in the bearing walls.'

So, he knew more than he was letting on about renovating his house, and about her, too. Somehow his hand had come to be tucked in hers. It felt warm and strong. She wanted to hold it forever. If such a thing existed. She yanked her hand away from him.

He looked at her innocently. 'I didn't want you to wind up with a nail through your foot.'

Leave now, the voice of her sanity dictated.

But Daniel was shamelessly playing her interest in old houses, showing her the intricate plasterwork in the ceilings and pointing out the fine wood wainscotting, the stain-glass in the upper window panels.

Why? the voice of her sanity chided.

'Come see this banister,' he said, leading her to a narrow staircase off the kitchen. She traced the age-darkened oak with her fingers, and let it draw her upward.

The stairs emptied into one bedroom. It was huge and bright, sunlight splashing across mellow hardwood floors. It was evident that Daniel had moved here from the hotel. The bed was casually made, and a shirt was on the floor. His suitcase was open on a chair beside the bed.

Well, now you're in his bedroom, the voice of her sanity said, with a certain resigned note. Flee!

But she didn't. She went over to the bed. 'It's beautiful,' she breathed, touching the brass reverently.

He didn't answer, and she turned to look at him.

His eyes had darkened to pitch, and her own breath quickened. She let go of the bed and started to move away from it. The room suddenly seemed too small.

'Want to test the springs?'

She froze, but he covered the distance between them. He stood very close to her, looking down. His hands moved to her hair. With one swift movement he had loosed the ribbon, and her hair tumbled free.

She snatched the ribbon from his hand. 'What do you think you are doing?'

'I hate your hair pulled back like that,' he told her unapologetically. 'This is how you should always look. Faintly wild, like you've just tumbled from a bed.'

His eyes drifted to the bed and then back to her face. The need in them was naked.

'Daniel, this has got to stop.' Her eyes had fastened on his lips. She remembered the taste of them. Her eyes skittered away, and hit the bed. That was even worse. She looked at the toes of her shoes.

'What?' He lifted her chin with the tip of his finger.

His touch sent a shiver right down to the core of her being. 'You know what! The suggestiveness.'

'The sexual awareness?' he growled.

'Precisely,' she agreed. He traced the line of her cheekbone with that same finger. She had to close her eyes against the sweet agony that his smallest touch stirred within her.

'I don't know how to stop it,' he breathed. 'How do you stop a storm? How do you stop the seasons? How do you stop water from running through your hands?'

'Daniel,' she said desperately, reaching up and grabbing his wrist so that sensual exploration of her face would stop. 'All we have in common is Kailey.'

'Really?' He lifted his wrist, with her fingers still entwined around it, and kissed her fingertips. His eyes were fixed wickedly on her face. 'It seems to me we have this in common, too.'

'Don't you see?' she asked urgently, her voice humiliatingly hoarse.

'I see perfectly,' he growled, his lips moving along the curve of her arm. 'I can't keep my hands off you. And you can't resist me.'

'I can,' she claimed, but there was a plaintive sighing sound in it as his tongue flicked the crease of her elbow.

'You can't.'

It was his utter male arrogance that finally empowered that nagging little voice inside her. Still, it took enormous strength, every bit of willpower she possessed, to pull her arm from his lips. She leapt back from him, afraid the arc of his passion would pull her back into his grip.

'I want you,' he stated simply.

She wanted him, too. Desperately. With a hunger so huge it seemed it would devour her from the inside out. She could feel the quiver inside her, her body and her soul whimpering for the fulfilment she had only ever found in Daniel's arms.

But she intended to be strong. Stronger than that hunger. She had something to prove to herself.

For the sake of her daughter.

'We can't be behaving like this if it's your intention to get to know Kailey,' she said through stiff lips.

'What does this have to do with Kailey?' he asked savagely.

'Aside from the fact that *this* made Kailey?' she shot back.

He reacted as though she'd struck him. His hands clenched into frustrated fists at his sides, and then he thrust them into his pockets. He looked away from her, out of a window that showed Copper Mountain.

When he looked back those dangerous lights had died in his eyes.

'You're saying it's untameable, aren't you? Wildfire. Out of control.'

'That's right. I don't want Kailey caught in the path.'

He stood very still, his eyes locked on her. 'You don't trust me at all, do you?'

She saw a chance to hurt him, and could not take it. 'I don't trust myself, either.'

'What a sad and lonely life you've come to lead, Annie. Everything under control. No adventure. No room for the unexpected.'

'I'm just doing what I think is best for Kailey.'

'And that's teaching her never to trust her heart? Never to take a chance on how she feels?'

She had taken a chance on Daniel once. 'Those things hurt. Those things can block out rational thought.'

'Yeah. Life hurts sometimes, Annie. And when you say no to ever being hurt, when you always make the rational choice, you aren't really living at all.'

She brushed by him, his words causing pain in her that she didn't want him to see. Life hurt sometimes, all right. She knew that. Because of him, she had already learned that lesson. In fact, she'd probably gone to the head of Daniel's pain class. She didn't need to repeat the lesson. She'd gotten it all the first time.

Who was he to tell her what living was about? Her life was full. She was contented. She didn't need the kind of messy complications Daniel represented.

'Annie.'

She paused on the steps and looked back at him, hoping her face was a mask.

'Did you come about the picnic?'

She had forgotten the purpose of her mission completely. 'Yes.'

'And?'

She never wanted to see him again. Not ever. He stirred up too many things inside her, not the least of which was the wonderful energy that sang and danced through her veins when she stepped this close to the edge.

Cancel. Tell him the forecast is for rain. Tell him you need to have a wisdom tooth extracted.

'We'll be ready at eleven, Sunday. I'll pack a lunch.' There, she thought, she'd shown him she wasn't afraid of his kind of power.

He smiled a slow smile that suggested to Annie that that wasn't the message he'd gotten at all.

'You can't hold back the storm, Annie.'

'Watch me,' she shot over her shoulder. She ran down the rest of the steps, through his house, and out of the front door as if the devil himself were chasing her.

The devil, who used temptation as his tool.

She noticed that her nipples were very hard under the prim cut of her ivory blouse.

'...and then Captain Hook takes out his sword and, SWOOSH, tries to cut off my head, but I pull out my sword and knock his wig right off——' Kailey's story stopped momentarily while she guffawed with loud self-delight '—and then I say, "WALK THE PLANK..."'

Around him, Daniel noticed that the woods were deep and silent, restful and serene. He tried to catch Annie's eye. She looked everywhere but at him.

'At least we don't have to worry about bears,' he muttered. 'Bears don't like noise.'

Annie had her hair pulled back again today, he noticed, and was wearing a baggy sweatshirt and severely unflattering khaki pants.

Not that she need have worried. He was determined not to let his hormones have the run of him today. It was embarrassing for a mature, successful man to be acting like a juvenile schoolboy. He wouldn't embarrass himself again.

Annie didn't deserve him. She'd had her chance. He had his pride.

'Are you listening?' Kailey demanded.

'Uh, I may have missed that last part,' he admitted.

His daughter glowered at him. 'That was an important part.'

'Is there going to be a quiz?' he asked drily.

Kailey stopped in the middle of the trail they were following and folded her arms over her solid little chest.

Her wild hair was held firmly back with a ribbon, something like Annie's.

'Do you think Hook would be a good name for a kitten?' she demanded.

'Only if it was a particularly foul-tempered kitten,' he responded.

She gave him a look that was something less than impressed and then, with a rebel yell that nearly peeled the skin off his ears, turned and ran up the path in front of them.

'Is it okay to let her go ahead?' he asked as Kailey's plump form disappeared around a twist in the trail.

'Fine,' Annie said.

He noticed that she was confining herself to one-syllable words, and still not looking at him.

'She's a little bit...loud, isn't she?' he said carefully. He could hear unearthly howls drifting back down the trail toward them.

Annie gave him a look that was less than impressed.

He wasn't sure how to interpret it, but thought it probably meant something like, 'Is fatherhood wearing a little thin so soon?'

He remembered what her hand used to feel like tucked into his, fragile and warm. He shoved his hands deep into the pockets of his hiking pants.

'How's the search going for a new house to raffle?' Answer that with one syllable, Annie Calhoun.

'Fine,' she responded.

'Well, what does that mean? That you've found one?'

'Possibly.'

He was clenching his back teeth together. Deliberately he relaxed them. 'Is "possibly" two syllables or three?' he asked. 'Do I detect an improvement?'

She shot him another look. It said clearly that she thought he was crazy.

There was a tightness in his chest every time he looked at her that confirmed that suspicion for him. What could be crazier than wanting a woman who had ditched you as Annie had ditched him? Not even a goodbye. A message through a friend, for God's sake.

Why on earth was he trying so hard?

Lust complicated things unbearably. Leave it alone, Starbridge, he ordered himself. Leave her alone. Get to know your kid. That's all.

A winter wren sang out, very close to them, and he saw Annie tilt her head toward the sound. Her eyes, those incredible turquoise eyes, sought the source of the sound and an unguarded smile tilted at their edges.

He didn't realize how much tension she'd been carrying within her until he noticed her mouth soften.

Leave it alone. What had he said to her? 'You can't hold back the storm.'

No? he asked himself. Watch me.

An hour later he was lying back among the litter of sandwiches. Peanut butter and jelly. Nothing special, Annie had told him coldly.

He wished he'd thought to bring the lunch.

Kailey, jelly smeared clear up to her ears, had grown subdued during lunch, her dark gaze darting between him and her mother.

'Did you guys have a fight?' she finally asked.

He looked quickly at Annie. 'No,' he said.

'Then why do you both have mad faces?'

'Do we?'

She lowered her brows and gave an exaggerated frown. 'Like this. This is how you look.'

'Ye gads!' he exclaimed, and hid behind a napkin.

Kailey giggled reluctantly, but wasn't quite ready to let go. 'Mommy, did you have a fight?' she persisted, apparently not prepared to take his word for it.

Two Calhoun women who didn't trust him, he thought glumly.

'No. Sometimes grown-ups just don't have very much in common.'

He schooled his face not to let her see how that little arrow had pierced the flesh close to his heart.

'But he's going to be your fellow, isn't he?'

'No.'

'Then why is he here?' Kailey wailed. 'If he isn't going to be your fellow, and you aren't even going to talk to him, why is he here?'

'I want to get to know you,' Daniel told her.

'Me?' Kailey's chest puffed up with interest.

'Yes, you.'

Her chest caved in. 'I'm not old enough to have a fellow.'

'No,' he agreed. 'But a friend, maybe?'

'You're way too old to be my friend. You could be——' A light of hope came on in her eyes that nearly blinded him. 'You could be my daddy,' she said tentatively.

For a moment the stillness was unearthly. The light in her eyes glowed with innocent optimism.

He looked swiftly at Annie. She had averted her head, left him to navigate the perilous ledges of his daughter's heart unguided.

'Would you like that?' he managed to ask.

She gave her mother a cautious look, seeking permission.

Out of the corner of his eye he saw her barely perceptible nod. He felt overwhelmed with gratitude.

Kailey planted herself firmly on his lap and wrapped chubby arms around his neck. She planted a small, infinitely tender kiss on his cheek.

'I've always wanted a daddy,' she confided in him. 'Even more than a kitten.'

'Ah,' he said, not trusting himself to speak.

'Course, I know it's just pretend, but it would be an ever so lovely just pretend, wouldn't it?'

He nodded.

'Daddy,' she said, softly and deliberately.

They both heard the muffled sound at the same time. Their heads swiveled to look at Annie.

Her face a taut mask, she got up, shoved her hands deep into her trouser pockets and walked away, her aggravation obvious in the set of her shoulders.

Kailey's face crumpled, and she disentangled her arms from around his neck and stood up.

'I'm sorry,' she said in a small, formal voice. 'But you can't be my daddy unless my mommy likes you.'

He nodded his understanding, fighting the lump in his own throat, feeling angry at Annie all over again. Why wouldn't she give him a chance?

'Could you make my mommy like you?'

'I don't know.'

'She likes chocolates and flowers.'

'I think it's more complicated than that.'

'Oh. Oh, well. Let's go pick some huckleberries. That might make her happy. We won't charge her for them.' A sticky little hand was held out to him. He took it and got to his feet.

He and Kailey picked berries, and ate quite a few more than they had picked. Suddenly he stopped.

'Kailey come here,' he called to her.

She came over, clown-like with the large purple ring around her mouth. She gazed down at the flower he had gotten down to look at. She squatted beside him.

'What is that?' she asked, her eyes round. She reached out.

'No! Don't pick it.' He arrested her purple-stained hand. 'It's called a fairy-slipper. It will die if you pick it.'

Kailey nodded her understanding and he released her hand. 'It's a wild orchid,' he told her. He had seen one only once before, and he was awed by its fragile, sensuous loveliness.

'It's bee-yoo-ti-ful,' Kailey breathed.

'You can make a wish if you want.'

'Can I?' She closed her eyes, and thought very hard. 'I wish for a kitten when Brook's cat has babies. I wish for one even though my mommy said no.'

He wondered what kind of trouble he had just gotten himself into now.

And then the sound came, soft and wild, eerie following so closely on his promise of magic. It felt as if his heart had stopped within the walls of his chest.

'That's my mommy singing,' Kailey told him softly.

'I know,' he said, just as softly. The wild, sad song did things to his spine. For a long time he and Kailey sat in the enchantment of the fairy-slipper, listening to the magic of Annie's untamed melody. Finally it faded, leaving an intolerable emptiness in its wake.

He handed Kailey back her pail, and returned to picking huckleberries himself. He whistled tunelessly, trying to fill a silence that had become too heavy. Annie did not reappear until late in the afternoon.

They presented her with their not very full pails.

'For free,' Kailey told her, and then whispered, loudly enough for him to hear and be embarrassed, 'Daniel really wants you to like him.'

'I like Daniel fine, sweetheart.'

He was surprised to discover that he did not want to be liked 'fine' by Annie. He would prefer her passionate hatred to such insipid emotion.

He glared at her. She looked balefully back.

Kailey gave them a troubled look. She was very quiet as they trudged down off the mountain. They were nearly at its base when she stopped short.

Turning, she began to run back up the path.

'Hold it,' Daniel said, catching her and swinging her up in his arms. 'Where are you off to?'

She squirmed in his arms with surprising strength. 'Put me down. I have to go back.'

'Kailey, it's too late to go back,' Annie said. 'We'll go again soon.'

'No-o-o-o-o.' Her shriek was loud. Tears burst out of her eyes. Her face turned a most unbecoming shade of red. She began to flail her arms and legs.

'We have to go back.'

'Why?' Daniel roared above her shrieks.

'I wasted my wish,' she managed to get out in enraged squawks. 'I have to go back and change my wish.'

He looked at Annie, who shook her head ever so slightly, warning him not to give in to her.

He set her on the ground when her wriggling was too much. She ran in circles. She stomped the ground. She lay down on it, pummeled it with her fists, and moaned as if she were dying.

'Kailey, that's enough,' Annie said firmly.

She was ignored. 'I have to go back or I will die. I have to go back or I will make you walk the plank. I have to go back or I will never be good again.'

'Kailey, that's enough,' Annie said again, her voice amazingly calm. She went over to Kailey, and a little fist connected with her face.

Annie gave a startled gasp and reeled back, holding her nose.

Daniel saw red. He moved swiftly, grabbed his daughter's arm and yanked her to her feet. He turned her and landed two good, hard swats on her bottom.

The screaming stopped abruptly. Mother and daughter stared at him with wide, astonished eyes.

'We don't spank in our house,' Kailey wailed, but there was very little spirit in it.

'No, we don't,' Annie confirmed, with a great deal of spirit.

He picked Kailey back up. She slugged him half-heartedly. He gave her a warning look and she surrendered, laying her head on his shoulder and closing her eyes.

He didn't glance back at Annie. Kailey's sobs petered out to gentle snores.

He got to her house, opened the door and went through to Kailey's room. He put her into her bed, pulled a loose quilt over her sleeping form. Her face was still splotched purple from her outburst and from huckleberries.

He was heading back out of the door when Annie caught up with him.

'How dare you spank *my* child?' she said, fight in her eyes as she folded her arms across her chest.

He stared at her. He felt furious. He felt as though he'd been put through a wringer-washer several times, and Annie, rather than looking the least bit sympathetic, was spitting righteous sparks at him.

'She's my child, too,' he reminded her. 'She needed a spanking and she got one.'

'What gives you the right, after being an absentee parent since her birth, to come into my life and think you are going to start calling the shots? I don't believe in spanking.'

'And it's bloody obvious, too.'

'What does that mean?' she asked coldly.

'What kind of mother are you?' he accused. 'You've turned that lovely little girl into a monster.'

He knew it was cruel, and probably uncalled for, but now that he had started there seemed to be no stopping.

He stomped by her on to the porch, but turned back. 'You're the mayor, the president of the Chamber of Commerce, the town entrepreneur, Copper's answer to Salvador Dali. When do you find time to be that poor kid's mother?'

He could tell that he was wounding her. But it felt good. It felt good wounding her the way she had wounded him. It wasn't as if he'd been an absentee parent by *his* choice.

She was beautiful when she was angry. Her hair seemed to hiss with electrical energy. Her eyes were stormy and blue and her cheeks blazed with color. It made him even angrier that her beauty could pierce his righteous anger.

'Why all the frantic activity, anyway?' he snapped at her.

She slammed the door so hard the glass rattled in its pane.

He wanted to go and pound on it until she let him in. He had a primitive urge to fight with her, and then kiss her with brutal dominance, and then take her to bed and have her.

But he'd seen the look of icy dignity on her face. She was never going to let him in.

Never.

And he could not know that she stood on the other side of the door, her back leaning against it, her body shaking with rage.

'Why all the frantic activity?' she murmured through clenched teeth. 'To try and fill the space you left in me, Daniel. That's why.'

CHAPTER SIX

ANNIE slipped into the church a little early. It was a tiny church. It had six rows of pews on either side of a red-carpeted aisle. The interior was finished in cedar and stained glass and now, in the early evening, the light coming through the windows was spectacular.

There were fresh flowers from Copper gardens at the altar, and their scent joined the scent of wax, wood and incense. It was a peaceful place. Annie had always found it a peaceful place. She went and sat in the front row and tried to lose herself in the colors and scents.

But it didn't seem to be working today. With a sigh, she opened her briefcase and took out some papers.

The back door opened, and in a moment Millicent joined her. Town and committee meetings were always held in the church because, small as it was, it seated the most people.

Annie gave her a tired smile.

'You look dreadful,' Millicent said bluntly, eyeing her critically over the top of half-glasses. 'What's the matter, Annie?'

'I seem to be having trouble sleeping,' Annie said vaguely. 'I'm sure it will pass.'

'Humph. Seen any of that Starbridge boy since Sunday?'

Daniel Starbridge was no boy, which was part of the problem. Annie seemed to remember his nature in his youth being far sunnier than it was now. When had Daniel become so disturbingly intense?

'No,' Annie said tightly.

'Humph. Maybe Kailey scared him off. He doesn't strike me as the type of man who could be scared off by a five-year-old child, especially his own child, but she could sour vinegar, that one could.'

'I don't think it's Kailey's fault he hasn't been around.'

Millicent looked at her shrewdly.

'It's only been three days,' Annie said defensively. 'I don't want him hanging around all the time, anyway.' Especially if he was going to accuse her of being a lousy mother.

'I'm sure you don't,' Millicent said soothingly.

'He does have his house to work on.'

'That's right,' Millicent agreed. 'Tell me, how long have you been having trouble sleeping? Since Sunday, perchance?'

Annie answered her with a glare. Thankfully the door opened again, and several other members of the house raffle committee came in in quick succession.

And then he came in.

The light filtering through stain-glass did marvelous things to his coloring. By some trick of the light he looked momentarily like the youth she had moments ago longed for—carefree and good-humored.

But then his gaze fell on her and the smile vanished from his lips, and that dark intensity—unmistakably a man's—was back in those dark, fathomless eyes.

She became aware of Millicent watching her with a small, satisfied smile on her face.

'What's he doing here?' Annie muttered in an undertone.

'Why, I invited him, of course,' Millicent said. She waved at him. 'Over here, Daniel.'

His easy smile returned for Millicent, and he came over. He said hello to several of the other committee members, and shook some hands. Everybody seemed delighted that he had come.

Paula, who owned the art gallery, leaned toward him and told him that she had had a new painting arrive, and asked would he like to come look at it some time soon?

Annie, who had always liked Paula just fine, was appalled to find herself disliking her suddenly.

What should it matter to her *who* Paula batted her rather thick tangle of lashes at? She was appalled for noticing Paula had thick lashes!

Millicent slid over and patted the spot between herself and Annie, inviting Daniel to sit.

Treacherous, meddling old woman, Annie thought, slamming her briefcase down in the empty spot.

Daniel picked it up, sat down, and settled her things on his lap. He looked as if he was considering rifling through them, and she snatched the briefcase from his lap and set it on the other side of her.

'I wasn't going to steal anything, Annie,' he informed her with faint scorn.

'Ha! I'll bet this is the first time you've seen the inside of this church,' she said to him in a low voice.

'Sorry, no cigar. In a town this size even devils like me get invited to the occasional wedding and baptism.' His voice lowered; his eyes held hers with embarrassing intimacy. 'How are you, Annie? I haven't seen you for a few days.'

The man would sound sexy ordering an extra pickle for his hamburger, she thought cynically.

'I'm fine,' she acknowledged him curtly, giving him a tiny nod and then deliberately focusing elsewhere. She was fine if it stood for frustrated, insecure, neurotic and emotional.

She sorted through her papers with grave care, then raised her voice above the cheerful drone.

'As you all know——' she opened the meeting '—Mr Starbridge——'

'Daniel,' he interrupted, giving the assembly his most winning smile.

'—has decided not to part with his late uncle's home on Elk Bugle Road, so tonight we need to look at our options. Does anyone have any ideas?'

There never seemed to be a shortage of ideas in Copper, though tonight, unfortunately, none of them seemed to have anything to do with the house raffle. Somebody asked Daniel what he did in Vancouver.

When he informed the committee that he owned Wild Melody, a faint, appreciative whistle pierced the sudden silence.

The awed shyness didn't last long. Someone else asked him how his parents were. And where he was staying. And how long he intended to stay.

Finally, exasperated by everyone's undisguised interest in Daniel, Annie interrupted.

'We really have only two options. There are two available properties that would be suitable—the old Beatlson place on Copper Mountain Road, and the Bailee house.'

The church door opened and Miranda scurried in. 'Sorry, I'm late,' she murmured.

Annie couldn't help but notice how pale she got when she saw Daniel. Daniel gave her a friendly smile—designed, Annie thought skeptically, to charm the socks off any woman under eighty. Or to reignite old fires . . .

But the smile seemed to fluster Miranda. She ducked her head, and sat in a pew across from everyone else.

Poor thing, Annie thought. She'd do well to remember that she wasn't the only girl in town who had lost her heart to Daniel Starbridge and had it tromped on by him.

'Personally, I think the Beatlson place is too remote,' Annie suggested.

'But the Bailee house would need a tremendous amount of work,' Daniel said.

'How do you know?' Annie snapped, and then flushed at the surprised looks her tone garnered.

'When I decided to keep my uncle's place I looked around pretty carefully to see what the other options for the raffle would be. I didn't want my presence here to be too disruptive.'

He smiled at Annie with such sweetness that she would have liked to knock his teeth straight down his throat.

'Gee, that was nice of you, Daniel,' old Clem Higgins said innocently.

Nice like a snake, Annie thought, watching him warily.

'The Bailee place may be beyond repair,' Daniel proclaimed, with irritating confidence.

'It is not!' Annie said. 'I went in it myself. It's very solid. The roof has leaked and caused a few problems, but nothing we can't fix. It has a beautiful yard, and with a little paint and plaster——'

'The foundation is crumbling. Short of jacking up the house and pouring a new one, that's pretty hard to fix.'

She stared at Daniel. She knew nothing about foundations, but she still resented his easy invasion of her territory. She disliked his taking over. She was well aware that sparks were hissing in the air between them, and that her fellow citizens were looking between her and Daniel like the audience at a Wimbledon tennis match.

'He's right,' Clem said helpfully. 'Foundation's a big job. I don't mind volunteering for a little fix-it-up carpentry, but I can't do that.'

'It would cost us a fortune to do that,' Daniel agreed.

'Us?' she said, through clenched teeth.

'Us,' he returned pleasantly. 'Now, I agree the Beatlson place is a bit out of the way but, you know, maybe we could market it as a wilderness retreat.'

Annie crossed her arms across her chest and tried not to let it show that she was fuming.

'I run a business that indicates very clearly the rising interest in outdoor pursuits. I know many of my customers would give their eye-teeth to have a retreat like Beatlson's. It's close to excellent hiking and fishing, surrounded by trees and mountains, a little creek right outside the door.'

'I think Daniel probably knows what the public wants,' Millicent agreed traitorously. 'That Wild Melody label is on every pack, sleeping-bag and jacket that comes through here. What do you think, Annie?'

'I think Beatlson's is too far out,' she repeated stubbornly.

'I went in and had a look at it,' Daniel said. 'The fireplace is magnificent. I thought we could take some pictures of the fireplace, and of that view out the front window, and show those wherever we sell tickets. And, speaking of selling tickets, I'd be glad to offer my Wild Melody chain of outdoor supply shops as ticket outlets.'

'Goodness, boy, you've got a good head on your shoulders,' one of the old-timers said approvingly.

Annie thought Daniel's head would make a good bowling-ball.

'Pardon?' Daniel said to her.

'Nothing,' she said sullenly.

'I've always liked that old Beatlson place,' Clem said. 'Wouldn't mind buying a ticket on it for my grandson in Calgary. He's a great hunter. Could use it in the fall.'

'Are we settled, then, on the Beatlson place?' Daniel asked.

Annie gave him a murderous look. The man was taking over her life. Wasn't it enough that she had to share her daughter with him?

'I still have some reservations about it,' she said stiffly. 'Perhaps we could have an expert look at that foundation.'

Her suggestion got her several black looks, as though she were dragging things out unnecessarily.

'I for one would like to decide things tonight,' Clem said. 'Got an itch to get going. We've already had a delay waiting to find out if this young fellow was going to sell his place.'

Millicent gave her a meaningful look when the word 'fellow' came up, as though this were some sign that she was destined by the heavens to have a relationship with Daniel.

Easily the most aggravating man she had ever met.

'Well, then,' Daniel said silkily, 'let's do it the democratic way. Shall we vote? Secret ballot or show of hands?'

'Secret ballot?' Millicent repeated, and everybody laughed as if Daniel were this week's winner of the comedy club. 'We just show our hands here, Daniel.'

'Sounds great to me. Keep it simple. For?' Daniel said, raising his hand high. A wave of hands went up.

'Against?' he said, grinning at her devilishly.

Stubbornly she raised her hand. She was the only one who did.

'Miranda,' he said gently, 'are you going to abstain?'

Annie looked at Miranda and frowned. She hadn't noticed Miranda's not voting, but she did notice that something was wrong. Miranda was trembling, and looked pale as death. Her eyes darted from Annie to Daniel and back again. Then, without answering Daniel, she clumsily squeezed out from the pew she had been sitting in and ran out of the church.

Daniel turned to Annie, the expression on his face genuinely distraught. 'What did I do?'

'I don't know,' Annie said, her troubled eyes still on the closed door at the back of the church. Miranda and Daniel had had some sort of thing, once.

Was Miranda's pain still as fresh as her own? Worse, had he had a reunion with Miranda like the one he had shared with her at Copper Hot Springs?

The thought made her stomach twist and her heart hurt.

'Miranda's just sensitive, is all,' Millicent declared. 'She probably felt as if you were asking her to betray Annie.'

Daniel looked stunned. 'But that's not what I'm suggesting at all.'

Isn't it? Annie thought peevishly. Still, if she was going to force herself to think rationally about it, she had to admit that Daniel's idea was pretty good. The towns-people had recognized that.

Had they also recognized that Annie was fighting him just for the sake of fighting him?

Suddenly she realized how childish she was being.

'The Beatlson place it is,' she conceded, with as much grace as she could muster. 'Now, we'll need to form committees. Clem, will you take the carpentry committee again this year?'

'Yes, ma'am. Be delighted,' the retired building contractor said.

'I wouldn't mind working on that,' Daniel said.

'The more the merrier.'

Several of the other men volunteered.

'I'll look after the interior cleaning, painting and decorating,' Millicent decided. 'And I'm sure we can count on Miranda to do the sewing for curtains and such. That gal is just a whiz with a sewing-machine.'

Annie volunteered to take on the publicity.

An hour later, buzzing with enthusiasm, they all headed to her shop, which she would open to serve them complimentary coffee and cake.

She trailed behind a bit, watching Daniel. The circle of the town had opened easily to include him. She could see he was liked and respected.

Of course, he'd grown up here. Some of these people had known him since he was a boy. It was his home town. Many of these people must have guessed that Kailey was his child, and yet there seemed to be no judgements. The town seemed willing to welcome Daniel back with open arms.

Would they do that if he was a total blackguard?

Maybe. They were simple people. Trusting. Willing to believe the best of people. Willing to give another chance.

That was the way they'd been with her when she had been a scared girl about to have a baby, with no one around to call her own. Her mother had moved on, but she had stayed.

And they had welcomed her, just as they seemed to be welcoming Daniel.

'Millie, can you look after coffee tonight? I have a splitting headache.'

'Little wonder,' Millicent said.

'Pardon?'

'You bang your head up against a brick wall, you get a headache.'

'I don't know what you mean,' she said stiffly. She wished, just occasionally, that Millicent would show her some of the deference she deserved as the older woman's employer.

'I mean, girl, that sometimes you got to quit fighting all those things going on inside you, and just go with them.'

'I don't know what you're talking about.'

'Humph. Well, don't expect to get a good night's sleep until you figure it out.'

Annie turned, unnoticed, up a side-street to go home. The evening was just growing dark.

Suddenly Daniel was at her side.

'Can I walk you home?'

For a moment she felt disoriented, as if she were being pulled backwards through a tunnel in time.

All those years ago, that was how it had started.

She had been walking home from a friend's house and suddenly Daniel had appeared at her side.

'Can I walk you home?'

She'd said yes. She'd seen him often over at his parents'—a wildly attractive boy that all the girls made a fuss over. She had been determined not to be one of those girls, and her knowledge of him was limited to the barbs they exchanged over the backyard fence. But, under the winking stars that night, it had all changed.

He had walked her home. Her heart had beat faster and her cheeks had flushed. It had felt so good to have that handsome, lanky young man walking beside her. It had felt so incredibly right.

As right as anything in her mixed-up young life had ever felt.

There had been no barbs exchanged that night. That night there had been a velvet silence as they admired the stars and listened to the gentle night sounds all around Copper. That night his hand had slipped into hers for the first time, and when they'd arrived at her house she had stopped and gazed up at him, and his eyes had been dark with surprise and wonder, as if he was seeing her for the very first time.

She wondered if he remembered as poignantly as she did. 'I hardly need a protector, Daniel. This is still Copper.'

'How about a companion?'

'No, thanks. Go have coffee.' *Maybe Paula will ask you over to see her etchings after.*

'I will. After I've seen you home. I wanted to talk to you.'

'I have a headache.'

'I know how to cure headaches.'

'I've asked you to stop doing that!'

'What?'

'Giving everything a sexual overtone.'

He laughed softly. 'As a matter of fact, I was thinking of a massage technique I learned in China. The sexual overtones are your own.'

She was glad of the darkness because her cheeks felt very hot. She was thankful that Copper was so small. Her house was exactly three minutes from downtown Copper. All those years ago the walk home had seemed too short. Tonight it seemed too long.

'Do you want to come out to the Beatlson place with me? It was the right choice, Annie. Wait until you see the fireplace.'

'I'll take your word for it.' Once, in that mad, exuberant summer, they had borrowed a cabin and made love in front of a roaring fire even though it had been nearly ninety degrees outside.

When she'd begun shopping for a house for herself and Kailey she had deliberately looked for one without a fireplace.

She didn't think that they were safe, she'd told the realtor righteously.

Crazy. One afternoon, and she'd never been able to see a fireplace again without sensing the danger, feeling the shiver of her own wanting. Which was just more proof that she was ruled by her passion, and that she needed to exercise rigid control over that wanton side of her nature.

The side that was even now noticing the scent of him, and thrilling to it.

'You know, Annie, if we're going to work on this house together——'

'We are not working on the house *together*. I'm on the publicity team. I won't even start my job until the house is nearly ship-shape. That could be several months from now. It remains to be seen if you will even be here then.'

He had been suitably vague when people had asked him about his plans for the future tonight. He was no more forthcoming now.

'Even if I go back to Vancouver I'll be coming back as regularly as I can to visit Kailey.'

The first part of the sentence seemed loud and clear to her; the rest faded into the night.

He was already thinking of going.

Just a few days ago, when he'd insinuated that his time here was limited, she had felt hopeful. Tonight she felt something different. A forbidden sense of loneliness.

He was getting to her. Despite her every effort, he was still getting to her.

'What about doing some before and after shots—if not for brochures, at least for the town's own records?'

'You and Clem go ahead,' she said woodenly. She had been in on every aspect of the other houses. She couldn't help herself. She had loved the process of reclaiming them, of returning them to dignity and usefulness.

She was going to have to avoid the Beatlson property as if the skull and crossbones had been hoisted above it.

She slid him a look. The skull and crossbones—and Daniel a modern-day pirate, pillaging hearts.

'Can I take Kailey for breakfast tomorrow? Do you think she's ready for me, one on one?'

She had just decided that she couldn't have Daniel around. She had just decided that she couldn't possibly have anything to do with him. Not with her emotions acting in such a treacherous fashion. So why did it feel, oddly, as if she was being left out?

'I'm sure Kailey will be enraptured.' She hesitated, standing in the light of her front porch. 'You weren't too put off by her behavior on Sunday?'

He came and stood very close to her. Without her permission, he reached down and took her face in between his two hands.

'I said some terrible things to you. I'm sorry.'

She ordered herself to pull away from the heat in his hands. But it was a feeble order, and her body mutinied against her mind.

'Forget it,' she told him, though she didn't intend to. She needed to keep a mental file of Daniel's transgressions to help her fight the temptation...of his hands.

His fingertips were lightly tapping her face, drumming down on it like gentle rain. She closed her eyes, suppressing a moan of sheer ecstasy at what the dance of his hands was doing to the knots of tension in her neck and her head.

She tried desperately to think of some of those transgressions. Her headache intensified, and with a sigh of defeat she surrendered to his ministrations. Score one to the buccaneers.

The motion of his hands changed, his fingers rubbing tiny circles on her temples, her cheekbones, her forehead. She felt so relaxed that she slumped slightly. He turned her, so that she could lean into him, while he massaged from behind.

It reminded her of a trust game they had played at one of the dozens of schools she had attended. Lean back, trust your partner to catch you.

Trust. The hardest thing of all. Even back then, all those years ago, she had never trusted him completely. She had grown up witnessing how transient an emotion love was. Her mother left the man or the man left her mother, but nothing lasted. Nothing stayed the same.

So even then, wild with love, she had tried to keep a part of herself from Daniel. She had watched the way women looked at him, watched the easy way he made them laugh, and she had known. He hadn't liked her friendship with Jeff Turner but she had stubbornly clung to it, knowing she would need Jeff's affection in the dark days when Daniel would go...

So she should know better now, but she did not pull away from those hands.

With the tips of his index fingers he sought out and found points in her forehead, on her cheekbones, in the center of her chin. He pressed them, hard. So hard that she thought she would cry out, but he always released the moment before the cry actually materialized.

His hands fell away from her.

She opened her eyes. Her headache was gone.

For a moment she stayed leaning against the wall of his chest, feeling languid and relaxed, watching the stars come out. After a moment she became aware that there was the tiniest of invitations in the fact that she was not pulling away from him.

She became aware that she wanted those strong, skilled hands to explore more than her face.

She straightened and swung around before he could even receive the invitation, let alone accept it.

'That's amazing,' she said with false brightness. 'Did you like China, Daniel?'

He looked at her for a long time. She could not read the look in his eyes, but she was fairly certain that it was not trust.

'No,' he finally said. 'I didn't enjoy China.'

'Why?'

His hand reached up and trailed over her face, then it dropped away and he shrugged. 'I missed this. Mountains, and silence. Space. But I also came to realize what a marketable commodity Canada's wilderness was. Good things come from bad. Sometimes.' He was silent for a time, and when he spoke again his voice was cool. 'I'll pick up Kailey about eight tomorrow, if that's all right with you.'

She hated that. She hated his forced attempt at politeness. She hated the strain between them. If the truth be known, she liked it better when they were fighting.

Passion, again. She was a throwback to generations of wild Calhouns, she supposed. She had inherited a fatal character flaw: a liking for things red-hot rather than luke-warm.

Crazily she wondered how much it would take to seduce him, to wipe that remote look from his face.

Crazy, like fireplaces in July.

Like falling so hard for a boy who was a leaver.

She was determined to leave all that craziness behind her. Her daughter would have something else for a role-model.

'Fine. See you then. Goodnight, Daniel.'

It satisfied her that her voice was about as exciting as week-old porridge stuck to the pot.

He turned and walked away. She stepped on to her porch and shut off the light. That way she could stand in the darkness for a long time, and no one would ever know that she stood and watched him until she could see him no more.

Crazy Annie Calhoun.

Daniel got into his car a little after eight. He had decided to take Kailey to Trail for breakfast. In his limited knowledge of children, he had somehow stored away the fact that kids liked McDonald's. He glanced at himself in the mirror and pulled the piece of toilet paper off his cheek where he had cut himself shaving.

He acknowledged that he felt a little nervous about having his daughter to himself. Should he ask Annie to join them?

The thought stirred a deep emotion in him, an emotion he had decided to resist. No, he would not ask Annie to join them.

It only took about a minute to drive from his place to Annie's, so he was stunned that both she and Kailey were seated in her ancient Volvo. He suspected that she would be long gone, except every time she turned the key there was an ugly grinding noise and not much else.

He got out of his car, feeling needles of anger jab at his stomach. He was ten minutes late and she was taking off? He had had about enough of Annie!

He went and yanked open her door.

'Where the hell——?' He stopped. Annie actually looked overjoyed to see him!

'Daniel. Thank God you're here.'

His anger vanished and was replaced by a flag of warmth unfolding in his belly. For the first time since he'd returned to Copper, Annie was glad to see him.

Or did that time at the hot springs count?

'Daniel, Brook has gone into labor. I'm her coach. I'm supposed to drive her to Nelson.'

Okay, so it wasn't him, precisely, that she was happy to see. She would have been happy to see anyone at this given moment. Still, he didn't mind this opportunity to play white knight to Annie's damsel. Not one little bit. Maybe she'd finally recognize that he wasn't the bad guy in this drama.

'Are we going for breakfast?' Kailey crawled over her mother and plopped out on the pavement beside him.

'How about if we go in Nelson?' he said. 'After we drive your Mommy and Brook to the hospital.' He could save McDonald's for another day. It never hurt to have an ace up your sleeve.

He transferred Kailey and Annie to his car and they drove to Brook's. He stopped the car in front of her neat cottage. He heard the most ear-piercing scream he had ever heard.

In the back of his mind, as he was sprinting toward the house, he realized that in his picture of himself as a white knight he'd envisioned himself carrying a suitcase while a very pregnant woman waddled down the walk in front of him. He'd thought about impressing Annie with his calm, speed and skill as he drove the curving road to Nelson...

He burst through the door. Nothing could have prepared him for what he saw.

Brook was lying on her living-room floor, her glazed eyes fixed on the ceiling, her face bathed in sweat.

And, unless he was very mistaken, she was about to have a baby. Annie came in right behind him.

'Dear God,' she said.

Daniel scooped up Brook and went through an open door into the bedroom.

'Don't panic,' he told the girl soothingly, tucking a clean sheet around her. His own heart was beating painfully hard within his chest. This was quite a bit more than he'd bargained for when he'd volunteered to be a white knight.

'Does this mean we aren't going for breakfast?' Kailey said, slipping in and staring wide-eyed at Brook.

'Kailey,' Annie said, 'run and get Millicent. I'll go phone the ambulance.'

Millicent, Daniel thought. Great idea. Ambulance. Great idea. What a woman Annie was. A knight couldn't ask for a better damsel.

Brook let out a terrified scream. Daniel took her hand and sat on the edge of the bed. He pushed the sweat-dampened hair from her face and smiled into her eyes.

'You're going to be fine,' he crooned. 'The ambulance is coming. Millicent will know what to do. Hang in there.'

Some of the terror left her eyes. She looked at him with trust. Her hand tightened on his.

'I'm so scared,' she whispered. 'I feel so alone.'

His eyes felt unexpectedly tight. Was this what it had been like for Annie? Had she been scared? And alone? Who had been there to hold her hand?

'I won't leave you,' he said hoarsely. 'You won't be alone.' And inside himself was a deep and abiding sorrow that he could not have been there for Annie when she had needed to hear those words.

It had been her choice.

Annie came back in with a stack of towels. 'The ambulance is on the way.' She went around and took Brook's other hand.

Daniel stared at her face. She looked beautiful, calm and tranquil. There was no mistaking her compassion for the girl, her genuine caring for her.

They exchanged looks over Brook's head. Annie gave him a smile that would have made a desert bloom.

And it felt as if that desert was his heart.

Of course, she had been here herself—a young woman with no husband to help her and support her.

It occurred to him that she had robbed him of one of the most special moments life would ever have given him. The blooms in his heart shriveled.

Millicent burst in the door, all angular efficiency. Daniel didn't know when he'd ever been so glad to see someone.

'Lord, love a duck, that baby is on his way into this world,' she exclaimed, 'and he ain't a-waiting for nobody.'

CHAPTER SEVEN

'OKAY, sweetheart, remember how we practiced it,' Annie said. 'Now. Push.'

Brook still had Daniel's hand in her grasp. Annie was certain that she nearly broke his fingers when she bore down.

'Good girl,' he encouraged. If his fingers hurt he was past the point of pain, so caught up in Brook's struggle that he could ignore his own discomfort.

Perhaps he had changed a great deal from the boy so engrossed in himself that he hadn't even bothered to say goodbye to the girl who had loved him.

It seemed fate was cruel sometimes. Daniel was so caught up in what was happening that he could ignore his pain. For Annie it was bringing a long-suppressed pain to the surface.

Daniel, whose name she had called over and over when Kailey was being born, was here for the birth of a different child.

And somehow he was everything she had yearned for in her own frightened young heart. How she had wanted Daniel there—holding her, encouraging her, welcoming their child to the world.

Instead he had been in China, learning how to cure headaches. And not even enjoying himself.

He had robbed her of one of life's most precious moments—sharing the gruelling glory of welcoming to this world the life they had created together.

She brushed away these thoughts. She couldn't afford the luxury of self-pity. Especially not right now. 'Push,' she instructed. 'Push, Brook.'

'There's his head,' Millicent cried.

'You're doing a wonderful job,' Daniel told the exhausted mother. His voice was calm and soothing, warmed through like hot brandy on a cold night. He brushed back Brook's sweat-tangled hair from her forehead. 'You're incredible.'

Brook gave him a tired smile. 'So are you,' she croaked gratefully. 'Millie, how can you tell it's a boy?'

'His ears. Sticking out like two jugs, just like Daniel's.'

Daniel touched an ear with exaggerated offense, and Brook giggled shakily.

'Push.'

'Arghhhh!'

'His head is out,' Millicent said, her face creased in a grin. 'The next one has to be a hard one, Brook, for his shoulders to come out.'

'I can't push any harder,' she whimpered, exhausted.

'I believe in you, Brook,' Daniel told her softly. 'You can do it.'

Annie noticed that, as tired as she was, Brook looked as if she'd go to the moon and back if Daniel told her she could do it. The girls had always looked at Daniel like that. And the Annie of her youth, full of insecurities because of her mother's gypsy life-style, had always felt faint disbelief that a guy like Daniel would choose a girl like her, forever.

'Push.'

'Hard, Brook,' Daniel commanded, all the gentleness gone from his voice, a football coach urging the best effort from his team. 'Harder. Harder.'

Brook responded. Her whole face, her every muscle and sinew, contorted with effort.

'Yes! His shoulders are out. The hard part's over,' Millicent informed the exhausted young woman encouragingly.

Brook sank back, shaking, dripping with perspiration.

'Did you hear that?' Daniel congratulated her, taking a damp cloth and wiping the moisture off her brow. 'Almost done. I am so proud of you.'

Brook's eyes rested on his face with an expression both tired and trusting. It would be so easy to soften your heart to a man who could inspire a look like that, Annie thought.

'Push.'

'He's here,' Millicent squealed. 'Lord, love a duck, he's here. He's beautiful.'

Annie laughed out loud. She had never heard Millicent sound so youthfully exuberant before. The dark cloud that had been hanging over her as Brook struggled, and Daniel struggled with her, dissipated as an indignant, thready howl filled the room.

Millicent, glowing to the roots of her gray hair, tied a lace round the umbilical cord, six inches from his tummy, and they lay him, slithery with blood, on his mother's stomach.

Annie looked at Brook's face. A light shone in it, soft and serene as candlelight. Brook reached out and touched her baby's slick hair. It was as though the world contained just the two of them.

Annie didn't want to look at Daniel. She wanted to look anywhere but at Daniel, but her eyes were magnets being pulled powerlessly toward steel.

Daniel was smiling, emotion glimmering in dark eyes that were fastened with awe on the baby. He reached out and touched the new child, his hand looking huge against the tiny form. Daniel's face usually had a certain unyielding strength in it, but now that strength was overlaid with tenderness.

She knew why she had not wanted to look at him. Because she had known that this was what she would see. Daniel at his very best. A Daniel who looked incapable of cruelty or selfishness. A Daniel who looked to be the dream every woman wanted: incredibly strong, but capable of deep sensitivity and compassion as well.

A Daniel it would be so damned easy to fall in love with.

She became aware that tears were tracking down her own cheeks. Tears of joy mixed with tears of sorrow. Tears for yesterday mixed with fears for tomorrow.

The doorbell buzzed urgently, but the people in that room were lost in a different world. They ignored it.

A Royal Canadian Mounted Policeman burst into the room and looked at them. 'I picked it up on my radio. The ambulance is only just crossing the Copper Creek Bridge now.'

Millicent looked at him and burst out laughing. A renegade chortle escaped from Daniel. Annie felt the bubble of laughter rising in her. The baby howled.

'He made it without any help from us, eh?' the policeman guessed, and moved over to look at the baby.

Even *his* features, Annie noticed, with his years of training in the fine art of being impassive, softened into a look of unadulterated tenderness.

Daniel rose, extended his hand and introduced himself.

'See this little lady here?' Daniel said proudly to the Mountie, gesturing to Brook. 'She's more of a man than you or I will ever be.'

The ambulance attendants arrived in short order. The baby was cleaned and the cord cut. He was wrapped in a clean white blanket. He had already lost interest in the world and was sleeping, his eyes clenched tightly shut, as Millicent, Daniel and Annie each had a chance to hold him.

Daniel seemed to have none of a man's uneasiness around the child. He took his turn with barely concealed eagerness, his movements sure and confident rather than awkward.

He likes babies, Annie thought, watching him, that bundle of life so fragile within the strong circle of Daniel's arms.

Of course, she reminded herself tartly, everybody liked babies. The reality of living with them was something else all together.

Brook and the baby were loaded on to a stretcher to be taken to the hospital in Nelson.

'Will you come with me, Annie?' Brook said, suddenly frightened.

'Of course I will.' In a way she was glad to be going. She did not want to be left with Daniel, the residue of magic, of tenderness, thick in the air all around them. This tangible softness seemed to affect her sensibilities nearly as badly as her passion did. 'Daniel, will you track down Kailey and keep her for a few hours?'

'Sure.'

Annie realized what she had just done. She had turned to Daniel first when she needed something. She had trusted him. A fist of anxiety closed around her heart.

'I left her at the shop,' Millicent said.

'Oh, by the way,' one of the attendants called as they wheeled Brook through the door. 'There's a cat having kittens on the couch.'

* * *

It was several hours later that Annie called Millicent, needing a ride home. Daniel volunteered to take Kailey and go and get her.

Once in Nelson, they stopped at a flower shop. He bought a huge bouquet of flowers for Brook. In truth he was a little worried that as a single mother she might not get much attention, that the arrival of her baby would not be celebrated in the way it deserved to be.

They progressed to the toy store.

'Kailey, you may choose a gift for the baby.'

Her chest puffed up proudly and she strutted importantly up and down the aisles, looking over every item with care.

She chose a G.I. Joe doll, who came complete with a sub-machine gun.

'Uh, this isn't exactly appropriate for a baby,' he said. 'How about this?' He reached for a large pink stuffed toy.

'That's stupid,' Kailey said. 'It's pink. Brook had a boy. Boys don't like pink.'

In this liberated age, were people still doing that? He found a blue elephant. 'How about this?'

'I want this,' she said dangerously, gripping the G.I. Joe package tightly. Her brows had lowered over her eyes.

'The baby won't like that, Kailey, he's just——'

'He will like it! He will!'

This last was said loudly enough to cause several people to look at them with interest and amusement.

'Kailey——'

'You told me I could pick, you liar.' Her voice was becoming very loud. He heard several snickers.

He closed his eyes, seeking guidance.

'Rat-ta-tat-ta-tat.'

He opened his eyes. G.I. Joe's machine gun was pointed right at his head. He made up his mind. Moving as fast as a cougar pouncing, he wrenched G.I. Joe from her tight little fist with one hand. With the other he picked her up, and tucked her under his arm like a football.

A very squirmy football.

She began to scream. 'This man is not my——'

He dropped G.I. Joe, clapped his hand over her mouth, and dashed for the door.

He opened the car and tossed Kailey in the back seat. She did not resume screaming when he removed his hand from her mouth, he noted gratefully. He reached across her and did up the seat-belt. She glared sullenly at him. She pointed her finger at him.

'Rat-ta-tat-ta-tat,' she yelled angrily.

He got in the car and drove, with her firing at him non-stop as they covered the short distance to the Kootenay Lake District Hospital.

He stopped the car. 'We are going in the hospital now——'

'Rat-ta-tat-ta-tat——'

'And you cannot make that noise in the hospital——'

'Rat-ta-tat-ta-tat-ta-tat.'

'—and if you do continue to make that noise, I am going to turn you over my knee and spank you so hard that you won't be sitting down for a week.'

The machine gun noises stopped abruptly.

'My mom won't let you.'

'Do you see your mom anywhere?' He was deeply ashamed of himself, not because he had just threatened his daughter with a spanking, but because of all the times he had looked on, feeling superior and judgemental, when he'd seen parents resort to spanking to control their children.

He'd already spanked her once, and he'd only been a parent a week. He supposed he'd better not aim for the Father of the Year prize just yet.

He watched Kailey in the mirror as she mulled over his threat. Finally, silently, she undid her seat-belt and got out of the car, marching in front of him like a defiant prisoner.

They found the maternity ward. They stopped at the nursery and looked at the babies. Daniel lifted her up so she could see. He pointed out Brook's baby, and then they went in search of Brook's room.

He had been worried that she would have no flowers. There was hardly a space to put his. Every single citizen of the town of Copper must have sent her flowers.

Had they done that for Annie, too? Annie, who was sitting beside Brook's bed, her loveliness shaming the radiance of the blossoms all around her.

He wished wholeheartedly that Annie had gotten fat, and wore glasses.

'I saw your baby, Brook,' Kailey said. 'I thought he was extra-ugly.'

'Kailey!' he exclaimed.

She turned around and stuck her tongue out at him.

'New babies aren't very pretty are they?' Brook said patiently. 'But, look, the baby brought you a present.'

Kailey's mouth fell open with surprise. She charged over to Brook and grabbed the package. 'I almost got him one, too, but he——' she sent a stormy look at Daniel '—wouldn't let me.'

She tore open the wrapping like a jackal going after a carcass.

Daniel stared in horror at the G.I. Joe doll, complete with a sub-machine gun.

Kailey smiled angelically. 'Just what I always wanted.'

She fell asleep as soon as the car left the parking lot.

'Thank God,' Daniel muttered, eyeing her in the rearview mirror.

'She must be pooped,' Annie said, glancing over her shoulder at her sleeping child. Her gaze was tender, all her strong maternal instincts in her face.

'Pooped doesn't say the half of it. She tried to get me arrested in Through the Looking Glass,' he told Annie indignantly.

Annie laughed, and reluctantly he saw the humor in it.

He laughed, too. 'So how come mothers have so much patience? Is it a gender thing?'

Annie didn't answer. He glanced over at her. She was as fast asleep as her daughter.

Both of them, sleeping, looked like porcelain angels.

And both of them, awake, were hell on wheels.

A week ago his life had been so blissfully uncomplicated. He felt his own exhaustion to the tips of his toes.

How on earth had Annie managed all these years by herself?

And how was she going to manage over the next few weeks with her sitter out of commission?

He wished it was none of his business.

He wished being a white knight worked more the way it did in the storybooks.

'What are you going to do for a babysitter?' he asked gruffly when he had stopped the car in front of her place and Annie had woken up. She looked flushed and vulnerable.

Kailey slept on, snoring softly in the back seat.

'I'm not sure yet. Brook wasn't supposed to have the baby for a few weeks.'

He hesitated. 'Annie, when you had Kailey, who was with you?'

'A friend,' she said quietly.

'I'm glad you weren't alone. I hope it was somebody who really cared about you.'

'It was,' she said softly. 'It was Jeff Turner.'

It felt as if she had taken a knife, twelve inches long and razor-sharp, and plunged it directly into his soul.

'Whatever happened to Jeff?' he asked, his voice a study in indifference. Damned if he was going to let her know that it had hurt then and it still hurt now, all these years later.

'He lives in Nelson.'

Why the hell didn't you ask him for a ride home? 'Oh.'

'He's Kailey's godfather.'

Yippee for him. 'Great.'

'He's been really good to Kailey.'

'Wonderful.' He'd stolen Annie, stolen a moment that should have been Daniel's and Daniel's alone, and now he was going to steal his daughter? Like hell.

'I'll look after Kailey until Brook is ready to start again.' His voice sounded grim, even in his own ears.

'Daniel,' Annie said with amazement. 'You don't know what you're taking on.'

'She's my daughter. Maybe it's about time I found out.'

'Daniel, I know you mean well, but——'

'Are you saying you think I can't handle it?' he demanded.

'I just think maybe you should give it some more thought.'

That sounded very rational, but for some reason around Annie his ability to be rational abandoned him. Totally. He was making a decision in the heat of the moment, and it probably wasn't a good one.

A roar that would have frightened a lion came out of the back seat.

Think about it, his rational voice urged him, for a week or two. By then it would be too late. Brook would be back on the job.

Jeff Turner would have had several more opportunities to be really good to Kailey.

'I'll do it.'

'Do what?' roared the lion in the back seat.

'Daniel's offered to look after you until Brook is ready.'

'I hate him.'

Annie shot him a look that invited him to change his mind.

He shook his head. He noticed he had a white-knuckle grip on the steering-wheel.

Annie came in through the back door of her house and set a sack of groceries on the table.

'Hello,' she called.

Daniel had been looking after Kailey for several days. He was doing a terrific job, even though it was very evident to Annie that it was nearly killing him. He looked a little more exhausted at the end of each day.

Today was Saturday, so he could have tomorrow off. In her shopping-bag were all the ingredients to say thank you to him. Thick T-bone steaks, garlic bread, potatoes, salad, a huckleberry pie with no fingerprints in it.

'Hello,' she called again.

There was no answer, but she could hear the television on in part of the house. She went into the living-room.

Kailey was lying on her belly, her chin in her hands, her eyes glued to the TV set.

'Hi there,' Annie said.

'Cowabunga,' Kailey said, without looking up from the *Teenage Mutant Ninja Turtles*.

Daniel was snoring softly on the couch. Several books were lying scattered on the floor around him.

Annie recognized them from her own bookcase. *Parenting. The Difficult Child. How to Talk to Children.*

A commercial came on, and Kailey got up and tiptoed over. She regarded her father's sleeping face.

'I covered him up myself,' she said possessively. 'He gets awfully tired.' She turned to her mother. 'I like him ever so much. Don't you, Mommy?'

'I thought you hated him,' Annie reminded her evasively.

'That was a long time ago,' Kailey said indignantly. 'When he said he'd spank me. He still says that sometimes, but he never does it.'

The turtle cartoon came back on, and Kailey lost interest in both her father and her mother very quickly.

If he had told her today that he was her father, surely Kailey would have shared that with her.

Annie went back to the kitchen. After a while Kailey came in, hungry and starting to act tired. Annie fed her, gave her a bath, and read her a story. Daniel slept on.

She put Kailey to bed and then popped the potatoes in the oven to bake. She put a lace tablecloth on the table and set it for two. She lit some candles. Then, in the soft light, she started making a salad.

After a while Daniel padded out, his feet bare, his hair tousled.

'What time is it?' he asked groggily.

She told him, and then swiftly turned her back to him. Something happened to her heart around Daniel. Especially seeing him like this. As if he belonged here. As if he was a part of their family.

'I didn't mean to go to sleep. Geez. What an irresponsible thing to do. Kailey could have burned the house down.'

Annie turned and gave him a quick, reassuring smile. 'It's okay, Daniel. I sleep. She gets up around six every morning, and hasn't burned the house down yet. She escapes, sometimes, and gets into mischief, but mostly of the minor variety.'

He suddenly seemed to notice the candles.

'Are you expecting company?'

The fierce note in his voice made her heart leap.

'I'm having company for dinner, yes.' She slid him a look.

His face had a very dark expression on it.

'I'm having you for dinner, Daniel,' she said softly. 'As a way of saying thank you for being such a big help over the last few days.'

The look on his face changed swiftly. She realized that it would have been much safer to buy him a card and a potted plant.

'What did you and Kailey do today?' she asked swiftly.

He told her about their day, and the sound of his voice, deep and mellow, tickled that sense of yearning within her. She sent him outside to grill the steaks, and then they sat down to eat.

'This is a wonderful treat, Annie.'

'I'm glad you're enjoying it.'

He snapped his fingers. 'I know what we need.' He got up and put some music on the stereo—soft music, that went well with candlelight.

She wanted to protest that it was too romantic, but who had started it, anyway? She had lit the candles.

She tried to defuse the romance by chatting about work.

Daniel watched her with dark, faintly amused eyes.

She talked about some repairs that her car needed.

Daniel's hand reached out and covered hers.

She talked about how the huckleberries were almost through for the year.

Daniel squeezed her hand, and she fell silent.

He stood up, her hand still in his. He bowed to her. 'Dance with me, Annie.'

She wanted to say no, but she could not, caught in the passionate web his eyes were weaving around her.

Slowly she pushed back her chair and went into Daniel's waiting arms.

He pressed her close to him and they swayed to the music. He buried his face in her hair, and she could feel his warm breath on her neck.

That ache was there. Oh, who was she fooling? That ache never went away any more. Because Daniel had become so much a part of their lives.

He was here first thing in the morning, his hair still damp from his shower. He was here last thing at night, a pleasant weariness etched around his eyes. Her house was full of his male presence, his vibrant laughter, his easy strength.

And her mind was also full of him. She did not escape when she went to work.

When she was young she had mistaken all this passion for love. Now she was a grown woman. Surely she could separate the two?

Surely, this time, she could slake her passion without giving away her soul?

What else would make this ache, the endless need, go away, except to satisfy it with his lips on her lips, the silk of his skin against the satin of her own?

She pressed herself closer to him, and felt the answering pressure from his hands. She lifted her head and looked at him, and he understood.

He took her lips with his, gentleness swiftly giving way to something far more basic. Need. Naked, hungry need.

He caught her face between his hands and devoured her, tasting every inch of its uplifted surface, nipping her ears, nuzzling her throat, plundering her lips.

With a ravenous and thoroughly shameless hunger of her own she returned his ardour—boldly, freely, holding back nothing.

Their dance now was nothing more than the sway of their bodies, thrusting against each other in the primitive age-old rhythm of time.

Then, with a cry of savagery and wanting, Daniel lifted her into his arms, his eyes questioning.

In answer, she took his lips again.

He carried her through to her bedroom, kicked the door closed behind them, and tossed her on the big pine bed. He stood for a moment, staring at her, his eyes pitch-black with passion as he looked at her hair scattered across the pure white of her pillowcase.

Above her bed was the painting. She had retrieved it from Paula's gallery and hung it where she'd assumed, perhaps naïvely, that he would never see it. His eyes caught on it, and he smiled with deep and possessive satisfaction.

He fell on the bed beside her, and kissed her with reckless inhibition. His hands trailed fire up and down her body, and then his fingers came to rest on the buttons of her blouse.

His eyes on her face, he undid the first of them.

She said nothing.

He undid the second and then the third one. Her breath was beginning to sound ragged in her own ears.

His hand snaked through the gap in her blouse, made short work of the fragile lace of her bra, and then she was gazing down at his hand on the ivory of her breast.

He traced the peak with his fingertips, then lowered his head to it. His hands dealt with the rest of the buttons and pushed the blouse back from her shoulders.

'Woman, you are so incredibly beautiful,' he murmured, his tongue raining fire on her waiting flesh.

While his mouth never left her skin, while she arched under the tender anguish of his kisses, his hands found the snap to her trousers, and it popped. Her zipper slid down, and the pants were slipped from her legs.

He rose above her. She was naked except for a scanty pair of lace panties. His gaze drank of her slowly.

Aware of the changes motherhood had wrought on her body, a sudden wave of shyness washed over her desire. She tried to cover herself.

He arrested her arms. 'Annie, you are so beautiful,' he assured her, sensing the sudden self-consciousness that was trying to dilute her passion. He lowered his head, and with a few well-placed kisses had fanned her desire back to white-hot.

'Undress me, woman,' he ordered her quietly.

Drugged, wanton, out of control, her frantic fingers trembled on the buttons of his shirt, pulled the tails from his jeans, eased it off the broad slope of his shoulders.

She dropped reverent kisses on the hard plain of his chest while her hands fumbled on the snap to his jeans. Finally it freed, and she opened his zipper and slid her hand through to the hard heat beneath it.

He teased her nipples to hard buttons as she tugged the jeans off him.

And then he was naked, save for low-riding navy-blue jockey shorts.

For a moment here was stillness as they regarded each other with heat and wanting, a volcano that had bubbled away beneath the surface for far too long, that needed to explode, that needed to vent.

It seemed nothing could stop what would happen between them, just as nothing had ever been able to.

'Annie,' he whispered.

'Daniel.' Her heart sang.

'Mommy,' a panicked voice shrieked. 'There's a monster in my bedroom!'

CHAPTER EIGHT

'THERE'S a monster in the next room, all right,' Daniel muttered. He rolled over, groaned, and pulled a pillow over his head.

Annie got up hastily and put on her housecoat. She went into Kailey's room. Kailey was kneeling on her bed, pointing hysterically at a spot on her wall.

'There it is,' she wailed. 'Mommy!'

Annie took a close look. 'Yes, I see it,' she declared. She went over, pretended to peel something off the wall, folded the imaginary monster carefully and put him in her pocket.

'Whew. Thank you, Mommy.' Kailey dropped back on to her pillow and shut her eyes.

'Any time,' Annie said drily.

She went back into her bedroom. Daniel looked deliciously sexy with the bright pattern of her quilt tucked around his bare chest.

'Come here, wench,' he growled.

She giggled, flipped back the covers and slipped under with him.

'What's this?' he asked with horror, finding her housecoat. His hands glided through the opening. 'And what's this?'

The housecoat came back off in short order. The heat built as his lips went over the path his hand had mapped.

'Mommy!'

A soft profanity came from his lips. He touched her hair, thwarted passion in his eyes.

'I need a drink before I can go back to sleep.'

'So get one,' he muttered.

But Annie didn't want Kailey up exploring the house. She didn't want to have to explain Daniel in her bed.

With a sigh she got up and put her housecoat back on, aware that Daniel's eyes watched her every move with burning need.

'Be right back,' she whispered.

'Right,' he said, throwing his arm up over his forehead and studying her ceiling, a look that could only be described as pained on his features.

'I'll hurry,' she promised.

Kailey, unfortunately, had a radar for a woman in a rush.

'Could I have a small smackeral?' she asked, after draining her glass of water.

'No!' Annie said to the snack request. 'It's the middle of the night.'

'Could I have a story? I'm not the least bit——'

'No!'

'Don't have to yell about it,' Kailey said, miffed. She pulled her blanket up and turned her back on Annie.

Annie went back into her bedroom. Daniel was sitting up. He reached for her. 'Okay, woman——'

'Daniel, she's wide awake. I can't. Not with her rustling around in there.'

'We could go into the living-room and turn the music on loud,' he suggested hopefully.

'I don't think so,' she murmured. Still, Annie felt torn between desire and duty. The very fact that she felt torn made her feel angry and ashamed.

As a child she'd become accustomed to the needs of her mother's latest man always coming first.

She wouldn't be the same as her mother. She wouldn't.

'Maybe you should just go now,' she said woodenly to Daniel.

'You don't mean that. I'll wait for her to go back to sleep. I'm not a complete caveman. I just want to be.'

Annie picked up a magazine and flipped through the pages, hoping he would get the hint to be quiet.

Instead, he groaned. 'I can't stay in bed with you for another second and not do something.' He sat up and pulled on his pants. 'Be back in a while.'

He stood up and tugged on his shirt. He left it unbuttoned. He looked like a poster of a virile, healthy, hot-blooded male. He tried to smile. It looked as if it came very hard to him.

She listened, her heart in her throat, for the slamming of the front door. She didn't hear anything. After what seemed to be a lifetime the tiny noises coming from Kailey's room stopped. Daniel did not return.

Annie felt rattled. She went and covered her daughter up, and then went in search of Daniel.

He was in the kitchen, his shirt now buttoned and tucked in. But would she ever be able to look at him again without seeing him as being unbearably sexy? He was standing at the stove. She noticed his shoes were on. Were her floors cold, or had he been debating leaving?

'I couldn't find anything stronger,' he said. 'I'm making some hot chocolate. Do you want some?'

'All right.' She flopped down at the table and pulled her housecoat tight around her.

'Kind of kills the mood, doesn't it?' he said. He was trying to sound cheerful, but there was a certain terseness in the words. He poured chocolate into two hand-thrown mugs and came over to the table.

He sat down across from her, and blew on his chocolate. He took a sip, and then set the mug down. His eyes locked on hers.

'Do all kids take this much energy, or is it just her?'

For five years she had done everything she could to be a good mom. Five lonely years of having the loudest child at every birthday party. Five years of having the most active child at every playground. Five years of tantrums. Five years of dealing with a child who would only wear three things and who would only eat macaroni and cheese.

'Well?' Daniel insisted quietly.

Annie didn't want him to see her loneliness and her confusion. The last thing she wanted from Daniel Starbridge was pity.

Because she hadn't figured out how to give her child the one thing she needed. Annie suspected that Kailey was a little girl badly in need of a father.

No, that wasn't quite accurate, she realized. Because Kailey was the child she was—demanding, difficult and challenging—Annie was a woman badly in need of a partner, a support system of love.

She didn't want him to see her vulnerability and she was deliberately cool.

'Kailey is very intense, but she's my daughter and I love her exactly as she is.'

'Are you insinuating that I don't?'

She knew they were going to have a fight. All this stormy emotion was thick in the air between them. It had been a mistake to go to bed together when there was too much unspoken between them.

'You want her to be like every other kid, and not all kids are the same.' She was going to fight with him about Kailey. It was dishonest in a way. Her anger was really about the fact that he had left her all those years ago, but she was too proud to say that.

'No kidding?' he said sarcastically.

'We seem to have this picture in our heads of what a child should be—happy, carefree, malleable, co-operative.'

'That sounds pretty good to me.'

'But some kids aren't. I've had to accept that. My child is not sunny-natured. She is not carefree, not easily managed, and is extremely strong-willed.' She sounded defensive and she knew it.

'Pig-headed,' Daniel said.

'That isn't helpful!'

'Well, what is helpful? That's what I'm trying to find out, Annie. How do you live day to day with Kailey and not feel so frustrated that about forty times a day you want to wrap your hands around her throat and squeeze?'

'Daniel!'

'I'm being honest. Is that more than you can handle?'

'I just don't expect it from you,' she shot back.

'What the hell does that mean?'

'It means why should I invest my time and energy in helping you get to know Kailey when you won't stay? When you'll walk away and break her heart when it all gets to be too much? There are cracks showing in the armor already, aren't there? She's not perfect enough for you.'

'That's not what I said,' he hissed tersely.

'Really? That's what I heard.'

'You know, Annie,' he said, and the anger was gone from his voice, 'I don't understand *you*, never mind Kailey. Every time we seem to get close, we end up fighting. What is it about closeness that scares you so much?'

He understood her a lot better than he knew, she thought.

'I don't want to be close to you, Daniel.'

'You're giving some pretty confusing messages, then, Annie. When you make dinner for a man and eat it with him in the candlelight, and dance close with him, and take off all your clothes for him, he gets this idea that you might want to be close.'

'That's not closeness,' she said sharply. 'That's sex.'

The blood drained from his face. 'You said once before that that was all we had. I'm starting to wonder if that's the only kind of closeness you're capable of.'

He got up, pushing the chair back so savagely it tipped. He reached over and slammed it back into place.

She wanted to tell him how wrong he was. How deeply she had loved. That she wasn't like her mother.

But tonight she had done her level best to seduce a man she knew she couldn't trust. And she should be thankful that the hand of fate had intervened.

But she was not. She felt empty, and devastated by his indictment of her.

She ducked her head. After a long time she broke the silence. Her voice came out in a croak. 'If you believed, all those years ago, that we had more than just sex, why did you leave?'

There was no answer.

She looked up. The kitchen was empty. She sprang to her feet and looked out of the window. Daniel was near the end of her street, his stride long and angry.

He had not heard her question. Suddenly, out of the shadows, another figure appeared. It was Miranda, and as Annie watched they stopped and exchanged a few words. And then unexpectedly Daniel put his arms around her and pulled her close to him.

Annie, her heart beating too fast and her eyes stinging with fury, pulled the Venetian blind cord so hard that it nearly came off in her hand.

Fate had intervened again.

'Are you and my mommy having a fight?' Kailey asked.

'No.' Fighting was preferable to the Cold War, he thought.

'You both have mad faces again.'

It was Monday morning. He had come to look after Kailey. He was a man of honor. He'd said he'd look after her and he would.

Annie had looked surprised to see him. That expression of surprise had lasted ten seconds or so and then her face had frozen up, colder than the tundra in January.

'Your mother wouldn't recognize a white knight if he hit her with his jousting-stick,' Daniel muttered.

'Huh?'

'This is a mad face,' Daniel said, furrowing his brows and curling his lip back off his teeth.

Kailey's eyes widened with admiration. She tried several mad faces of her own.

He hoped the matter was dropped, but of course he should have known better by now. His daughter was nothing if not persistent.

'My mommy looked very sad all day yesterday,' Kailey confided in him.

'Did she?' It was her own darn fault.

'Yup. She went into the bathroom and cried.'

'How do you know?' The thought of Annie crying in the bathroom was a little more retribution than he wanted.

'I could hear her,' Kailey said. 'I yelled through the door, "Mommy, what's wrong?" and she lied at me and said "Nothing".'

'She just doesn't want you to worry about her.'

'Well, I worry about her all the time.'

'You do?'

'It must be lonely being a growed-up with a kid. Especially a kid like me.'

'What does that mean?' he asked carefully.

She turned her huge dark eyes on him. 'I'm not a good kid, you know.'

'Aren't you?'

'No. I try and try, but I do have bad behavior.'

'Sometimes you do,' he acknowledged.

'Like that time in the toy store,' she said sorrowfully. 'Can I tell you a secret?'

'Sure.'

'I didn't want the G.I. Joe for the baby. I wanted it for me. I thought, I'll buy it for the baby, and he won't like it, and I'll get it.'

'You know, Kailey, because you do bad things sometimes doesn't mean you're a bad girl.'

She rolled her eyes. 'Now you sound just like my mom.'

'Because we both know that's true.'

'Anyway, I can't stop being bad. I tried and tried. Sometimes the days I try the hardest, I be the baddest. I be good, and good, and good and then, BAM—all the bad comes rushing out.'

Her face was very solemn. He stifled a laugh.

'You know what, Kailey, I think, as you get older, you'll just sort of grow out of doing bad things. That's what happens to most of us.'

'Were you a bad boy?' she asked eagerly.

'Sometimes.'

'Ooohh,' she breathed eagerly. 'Could you tell me all about it? Did you ever tie a cat's tail to a fence?'

'Er, no.' He looked at her suspiciously. 'Have you?'

She nodded. 'Tried. It didn't work. What did you do that was bad?'

He was almost afraid to tell her. It might be like giving a pyromaniac matches. 'Once I painted a white garage with tar that a road crew had left out.'

'Did your mom cry?'

'My dad spanked me.'

'Precisely,' Kailey said with satisfaction.

'Precisely?'

'That's why I think my mommy should marry up.'

'Marry up?'

'I need a daddy, then Mommy wouldn't feel so re-prensible all the time.'

'Responsible?'

'Precisely. She'd have another growed-up to keep her company.'

'Do you have somebody in mind?' he asked cautiously.

'You know I do,' she scolded him. 'You.'

'Me? I think there must be people she likes better than me. How about Jeff Turner?' He felt immediately ashamed of himself. It was not very ethical trying to pry information from a five-year-old.

'Uncle Jeff? You silly. He's already married up.'

'He is?' His heart seemed to leap within his chest.

'He has an extra-ugly baby just like Brook's, only it's a girl.'

'He does?'

'And she didn't bring me a present.'

'That's too bad.' A new baby must mean things were pretty solid between old Jeff and his wife.

'So, should we go ask Millicent how you can woo my mommy, or should we just go and buy her some chocolates and flowers?'

'Let's go with the chocolates and flowers.'

Kailey beamed at him. A sticky hand found its way into his. 'I'll probably get to eat most of the chocolates, you know. My mommy doesn't like to get fat.'

He came across the idea like a miner who had been digging and clawing his way through endless rock and gravel and dirt. Suddenly he saw it—a band of pure gold, running through all the rocky terrain he had crossed with Annie.

Kailey was absolutely right.

Annie needed to marry up.

The idea danced within him—shining, sparkling with glimmering brilliance out from under all the muddy confusion and frustration. He'd never stopped loving Annie, though Lord knew he had tried for six long years. He had never succeeded. And he probably never would.

She needed him. She needed a man—to talk to, to laugh with, to love.

To love. Now that was the tricky part. Annie didn't want to love him. Love was too much for her. That was probably really why she had left him for Jeff Turner six years ago.

The feelings were too intense for her. Too sweet. Too drugging.

He remembered Annie's mother. She'd been a beautiful woman, very much like Annie in appearance, except where Annie was earthly her mother had been worldly.

Very worldly. She'd worn too much make-up. Her dresses had been too high at the hem and too low at the neck.

She'd dragged Annie from town to town, chasing this man and that, teaching Annie a warped lesson about love.

So when Annie had fallen in love herself it must have scared her near to death, Daniel decided unhappily. And it was scaring her near to death again.

He knew what he had to do. He'd ask Annie to marry him, but he wouldn't mention love.

He'd talk about Kailey and how much she needed a father. He'd get his foot in the door. That was what he would do. And, in time, that abundance of love that shone in Annie would be freed, and would come tumbling out all over him. In time she would learn to trust, not just him but her own feelings.

He wanted to be Annie's husband.

'You whistle real good, Daniel, almost as good as my mommy sings.'

He realized that he was whistling that same haunting, untamed melody that was Annie's. When had he learned how to do that?

'Could you teach me?' Kailey puckered up her lips and blew.

He grinned. 'Sure, sweetheart. Right after we get the flowers and chocolate.'

'Sorry I'm so late,' Annie called. 'The delivery van that takes the pastries to Castlegar was late.' There was no answer.

She walked through to the kitchen, bracing herself to see Daniel. Even when she was angry with him seeing him always filled her with momentary warmth, yearning. She reminded herself of how he'd gone straight from her arms to Miranda's. The very same way he had six years ago.

Kailey and Daniel were sitting at the table, playing a board-game. They both looked up at her and smiled grins that seemed too large. Something was wrong, she thought suspiciously.

They both looked fresh-scrubbed, and Kailey was in her red dress. The one with the pinafore and puffy sleeves that she hated.

Daniel looked more casual, but very crisp in a coffee-with-cream-colored chambray shirt. Unless she was mistaken, his jeans had a freshly ironed crease down the center of each leg.

'Okay, you two,' she said, placing her hands on her hips, 'out with it.'

'Out with what?' they both protested innocently.

She studied them for a few minutes. They had both gone back to the board-game. Kailey giggled. She looked flushed.

'What's that smell?' She turned to the counter. A dozen pure white roses had been arranged in a cut-glass vase.

'Pizza,' Daniel said blandly. 'I bought pizza for supper tonight.'

The roses threatened to dazzle her. Almost against her will, she went over and touched one of the perfect petals. She buried her nose in one.

Her eyes caught on the box beside the roses. Chocolates. A huge box of very good chocolates, tied neatly with a white ribbon.

'Okay, you two,' she said sternly, folding her arms over her chest and turning back to them. 'What's going on here?'

But there weren't two any more. There was just one. Daniel.

'Where's Kailey? What has she done?'

'Nothing, Annie. She went to play in her room for a while.'

'What's this all about, Daniel? Roses, and chocolates, and pizza?'

'I was trying to create a mood.'

Well, he had succeeded in creating a mood, she thought, but probably not the one he wanted. She felt tense with wariness.

'What for?'

He got up from his chair and came over to her. He looked down on her and smiled.

She could have read a lot of tenderness and caring into such a smile if she were the naïve young girl she once had been.

'It's about this, Annie.' He fished in the front pocket of his shirt and pulled out a tiny box.

She stared at it. She made no move to take it.

Unperturbed, he opened the box and took a ring out. A dainty ring, flashing gold in the fading light of her kitchen, and winking with bright white diamonds.

He picked up her nerveless hand and slid the ring on her finger. It fit perfectly.

She gawked at it. It seemed as if her heart had stopped beating, and as if there was no breath in her.

It was the most beautiful ring she had ever seen.

'I want you to marry me, Annie.'

The words were deep and soft. She could not look at him. She turned from him, but there was no place to run. She was hemmed in between him and the counter. She grasped the edge of the counter and watched her hands turn white. It made the ring look all the more beautiful.

His hands were on her shoulders, massaging away the tension.

Those hands that could talk her into anything.

'Annie, I know I've caught you off-guard, but if you think about it this is the best thing for us. For Kailey. Kailey needs a father. She desperately needs a father.'

Annie closed her eyes against the pain rising up within her.

For one star-strewn moment she had thought the ring had meant that it was true.

That all those years ago when he'd said those words 'I'll love you forever', he'd meant them. That he'd tried to outrun his feelings and could not.

For one moment she had hovered on the edge of paradise.

And he had taken it away from her. Again.

She would not marry Daniel so that he could be the father to her child, not even if that was what Kailey needed most.

'Annie, think about it. It would be good for Kailey. But it would be good for us, too.'

She said nothing, struggling with her pain. It sounded as if he was making a business proposition. That would be like Daniel. Then he could be married and free, both.

'I know how to cure headaches,' he reminded her.

His tone was so light, so irreverent. Now he was going to make jokes about it.

Thankfully the humor left his voice.

'As a man and a woman,' he said softly, 'we have certain needs——'

That was the last straw! He was *not* going to use the fact that she was physically so vulnerable to him, the fact that she was so much like her mother, to talk her into this.

She whirled around and twisted his ring off her finger.

'I wouldn't marry you if you were the last man on earth,' she snarled, mustering all the harshness she could to mask the hurt unfurling in her like an endless flag.

'Annie——'

'Never.'

'Annie——'

She thrust the ring into his hand, closed his unwilling fingers around it.

It had been a mistake to touch him. Just say yes, a voice inside her wailed desperately. Does it matter how you have him, just so long as you have him?

Yes. It mattered. Furious with her own weakness, she shoved at the hard wall of his chest.

'Go away. Get out of my house. And don't you ever come back.' She felt furious. Would this man ever stop hurting her?

His own features looked absolutely impassive to her, devoid of emotion. But then this latest ridiculous scheme wasn't about emotion. It was about need. He turned away from her. And stopped with an abruptness that made her peer over his shoulder to see what had stopped him.

Kailey stood in the kitchen doorway, her face white and anguished, silent tears running down her face.

It was the silence that cut through Annie like a knife.

Kailey's small shoulders slumped inside her pretty dress, and her head fell forward. She looked like a tiny, broken doll as she turned and shuffled away from them back toward her room.

Annie rushed past Daniel. She gave him a contemptuous look over her shoulder. 'Look what you've done,' she spat.

His chin went up at a haughty angle and his eyes burned into her. 'What I've done?' he said softly. 'Look what you've done, Annie Calhoun.'

Annie went down the hall, just in time to see the bathroom door slam shut and to hear the lock click.

'Kailey, let me in.'

'Need to be by myself,' a tiny, shattered voice came back. 'Leave me alone, Mommy.'

The back door slammed. Annie sank down, her back pressed against the hallway wall. She lowered her head on to her upraised knees and closed her eyes against a pain so acute it felt like hot coals within her.

What have you done, Annie Calhoun?

Daniel tried to walk the fury out of his system. Lord, that woman made him so angry.

He pulled a deep breath of the cool air into his lungs. Fall was fast coming to Copper. Soon the huckleberries would be gone, and the green of the leaves would change, painting the mountainsides shades of yellow and red and gold.

It was about this time of year that he had left Copper.

And there was no doubt about it; he was thinking leaving thoughts again.

She hadn't just said no. She had scorned him.

The same as last time.

He felt like ten kinds of a fool. He'd just let history repeat itself.

He'd fallen in love with that baffling, infuriating woman all over again, and let her do the very same thing as last time.

At least this time she'd scorned him to his face instead of leaving a message with a friend.

Last time she'd said that she was too young for forever.

But the truth was something different. Annie wasn't the forever kind.

Yes, he'd have to leave Copper.

He was mildly surprised by the pain that caused in him. He felt at home here. It was a feeling he'd looked for in all his travels, a feeling he had tried to get in Vancouver and never had.

Copper was where his heart was.

But he couldn't stay here.

The pain of loving her had never quite gone away, not even with six years and three hundred miles separating them. But at least it had been a dull pain, somewhere in the background of a life he'd deliberately made too busy.

Here the pain was unbearable.

It seemed to tear at his chest and claw at the back of his eyes.

He let the fury wash back over the hurt. He walked and walked and walked. Then he went home and began to throw things into his suitcase.

First thing in the morning, he'd be gone.

He realized that he'd miss Kailey. He didn't want to go without saying goodbye to her, but he couldn't see Annie again. He wanted to leave with some of his dignity intact.

That cold-hearted, unfeeling woman. What kind of man fell for a woman like that, anyway?

Kailey, he reminded himself. He'd leave her something special, and then call her from Vancouver every day.

He knew exactly what to leave her. One of Brook's kittens. He smiled grimly. Perfect. Kailey would love it. Annie would hate it. Every time she looked at that kitten she would think of him and be angry.

Good. If she wasn't prepared to love him, at least he could leave a reminder of himself around to irritate her, to make her think of him every day.

His decision made, he pulled on his jacket and went back out of the door. He walked down to Brook's house. He could hear the squalling of the baby inside.

When Brook opened the door she looked tired and radiant.

'Daniel, I'm so glad you came.'

Oddly enough, he was, too. Brook gave him the baby and a heated bottle.

The baby's weight felt warm in his arms, and a sweet scent came off the child. He drank lustily, his fierce gaze fixed unwaveringly on Daniel's face.

If she had said yes, they might have had another baby.

Hastily he handed the baby back to Brook.

'I have to leave tomorrow,' he said.

'What? No! Daniel, don't go.'

'I have to,' he said evenly. 'I came to arrange to have one of the kittens for Kailey.'

Brook looked at him thoughtfully. 'Are you Kailey's father?'

He nodded. He had wanted to give Kailey that moment, when he could tell her that he was her father, like a carefully wrapped gift.

Another thing Annie had stolen from him.

He wouldn't see her in person again for a long time.

'Annie already made it quite plain to me that Kailey was not allowed to have a kitten.'

'I need to leave her something, Brook, something extra special. I'm trusting you to see that she gets the kitten.'

'All right,' Brook said with a sad smile. 'Come and pick one.'

He went over to the basket. The kittens were beautiful now, fluffy and plump and soft.

One was completely white with two black circles around its eyes. It looked like a little outlaw. The perfect pet for his little outlaw.

'That one,' he said softly. He wished he could be there to see her face when she got it. She'd been such a good girl, not asking once for any of the kittens even though it was so evident that she wanted one so badly.

He left Brook and wandered up the streets of Copper for the last time.

Finally he managed to exhaust himself.

He went home and went to sleep.

In the morning he took a last quick look around the house. He packed away his shaving gear without using it.

He snapped shut his suitcase.

Somebody knocked on the door.

He opened it to Annie.

For one crazy, hopeful moment he thought she'd changed her mind.

'Daniel, is Kailey here?'

'No,' he said grimly, folding his arms over his chest.

'Daniel.' Her voice broke. 'Kailey is missing.'

CHAPTER NINE

'ANNIE, come in.'

She was aware that she was shaking. It pierced her panic that the cold look was gone from Daniel's face.

She stepped in his door. Her mind insisted on registering silly details. Daniel looked haggard. His whiskers were unshaven and his shirt was rumpled. She looked away from him. The house was starting to look good. Then she saw the set of suitcases, bulging the way that suitcases ready to go did.

'What do you mean Kailey is missing?'

Worry-lines had creased the sweep of his forehead. His love for Kailey was naked in his face. With her panic building since seven this morning she had felt increasingly alone.

She was with the one other person on earth capable of loving Kailey as much as she did.

Now she didn't feel alone any more.

Her eyes drifted to the suitcases, and she thought of that strange embrace she had witnessed between him and Miranda. Maybe it was just an illusion, but she needed something to cling to. She took a deep breath.

'When I got up this morning she wasn't in the house. I've phoned all the places she usually goes. I was hoping she was here.'

'I would have called you if she came by here unexpectedly.' There was gentle chagrin in his tone. He was telling her that he did the right things, to trust him.

She realized that some time in the past few weeks she had come to trust him with Kailey. She knew his relationship with his difficult daughter was magical and special. She knew he wasn't going to hurt Kailey the way he had hurt her all those years ago.

He would never be able to leave Kailey without so much as a backward glance. Well, blood was thicker than water.

But the scene she had witnessed and the packed suitcases at the door would not allow her to trust him for herself.

So he was leaving.

She had always known this moment would come. Why did it feel like this? As if one person she loved was missing and another was ready to go, and that the bottom was falling out of her carefully structured world?

'Where could she be?' She could not disguise the fear in her voice.

He stepped toward her. She shrank back from him. If he touched her she might fall apart.

He hesitated, but then, looking steadily at her face, came ahead. He put his arms around her, just as she had seen him put his arm around Miranda. 'We'll find her.'

She did not fall apart. Instead she found surprising comfort in his arms. Her own strength felt as if it was fast fading, and she needed his. Temporarily.

'I'm scared, Daniel. It's not like her. I mean, she does slip out and get into all kinds of mischief, but she's predictable. She goes to the shop, or to Brook's, or to steal a few flowers from Millicent's garden. She doesn't disappear. And she doesn't leave notes.'

'A note?' Daniel asked. She could hear the relief in his voice. He still had so much to learn about children.

She stepped back from him and pulled the grubby sheet from her pocket. She smiled shakily as she handed it to him.

He took it and unfolded it hastily. His eyes scanned it. Annie already knew it by heart.

DEAR MOM:
SSSTTYKllmmmmopPOOp.
KAILEY.

A reluctant smile teased the corners of his worried mouth. 'Thanks a bunch, Kailey.'

'What am I going to do?'

'What are *we* going to do?' he corrected her softly.

She nibbled her lip. 'Yes, we.' She had thought it would be hard to say, but it wasn't. It felt as if an enormous burden had been lifted from her shoulders. It felt as if finally, after all these years of toughing it out alone, someone cared with her.

The light in his eyes as he looked at her so gravely would make it very easy to believe that he cared for her, too.

He looked away from her to his watch. 'It's only eight. Why don't we go door to door? She's gone in visiting somewhere and forgotten to tell you, that's all.'

'She wouldn't. She knows she's not allowed to go in to strangers.'

'Annie, does anybody in the whole town qualify as a stranger?'

'Daniel, have you ever heard of mother's intuition?'

He nodded.

'Something's wrong.' Kailey had been upset last night. She had cried herself to sleep, inconsolable.

Annie had felt fairly inconsolable herself. She had wondered if a piece of Daniel wouldn't have been better than no Daniel at all.

She looked at the chiseled handsomeness of his features. No, she did not want a Daniel who did not love her exclusively. If she had wanted that she could have told him about his daughter a long time ago.

'Why don't we get everybody we know knocking on doors or making phone calls? You stay home in case she comes back.'

'I can't stay there by myself.'

'Millicent can stay with you.'

She wanted Daniel to stay with her. She did not want to let go of him. There was a bond between them, and it seemed to be more than the fact that they shared a child.

Sometimes it seemed they shared a soul.

But then it had always seemed like that to her. What it seemed like to him, she couldn't even guess.

'Yes,' she agreed. 'Millicent can stay with me.' She could see that he would not be able to sit still, and she could see that the pressure she was under right now could easily crack the carefully constructed façade of indifference she had put up around herself where Daniel was concerned.

It was noon when he came back to her house. She had never spent four hours in such helpless misery. When she heard his familiar tread on the front steps hope leapt in her breast. But the moment she saw him she could read the answer on his face.

She had never felt anything like the fear that billowed up in her stomach in a great, suffocating dark cloud. She put her head in her hands and wept.

He came and sat beside her for a moment, his hands stroking her hair, soothing words coming over and over again off his tongue.

'I'm going to call the police,' he finally said, pulling away from her.

'Oh, Daniel.'

'I should have done it right away, Annie. I just couldn't believe...' His voice trailed off.

'I know. Calling them makes it so real.'

'It is real.'

She nodded through her tears. It was a nightmare, but she wasn't going to wake up. It was real.

Daniel came into the living-room a few minutes later and sank back down on the couch. He rested his elbows on his knees and put his head between his hands.

His despair made it even more real.

'Now, now, you two,' Millicent said, coming into the room. 'She's just gone wandering, that's all. Children do that.'

But even Millicent sounded afraid. She turned back out of the room abruptly. 'I'll start making sandwiches and coffee.'

Daniel and Annie both looked at her.

'For the search parties,' she said softly.

A knock came at the door, and they both jumped up to get it.

Miranda stood on the porch. 'You're both here,' she whispered. 'Good. I need to talk to you.'

'About Kailey?' Daniel's voice was raw with hope.

'Kailey?' Miranda echoed, puzzled. 'No, I wanted to straighten things out about the other night. What about Kailey?'

'She's missing,' Annie said wearily, the hope that had temporarily lit in her dying abruptly. 'She's been missing since this morning. What about the other night?'

Even with her daughter missing she was horrified to find that she was inspecting the expressions on Daniel's and Miranda's faces to see what was passing between them. She came up empty. Surely people who shared a passion looked at each other... Well, like she and Daniel looked at each other.

'That doesn't matter now,' Miranda gasped. 'What can I do? Tell me. I'll do anything.'

No, whatever had happened between them the other night did not matter now.

'Come and make sandwiches,' Millicent ordered from the doorway.

Daniel got up restlessly and went outside and stood on the porch, his eyes scanning the street, searching the hills as if they would give him answers.

Annie went and stood beside him. She wanted to touch him, and in her pain she saw no reason to deprive herself.

When she reached out her hand he pulled her swiftly into the side of his chest; his arm went tightly around her shoulder. With a sigh, she lay her head on his shoulder.

Two people, comfortable together at last, their suffering tearing down some terrible barrier between them.

'Annie, she wouldn't go for huckleberries by herself, would she?'

Annie started. Her eyes flew to where the huckleberry pails were neatly stacked in the corner of the porch. The little red plastic one with the white handle was gone. 'Yes! Daniel, she might. I mean, I've told her a thousand times, but you know Kailey.'

'Not nearly as well as I want to.'

He had barely had a chance to know her. If anything happened to her, Annie thought, he would feel robbed, so robbed.

And so would she.

'Let's go,' he said, leaping off the porch without hitting a single stair, just the way he had all those years ago when he had been an exuberant youth with too much energy...and too much charm.

But the face he turned back to her had aged a hundred years since he had opened his door this morning.

'Wait.' She went and gave quick instructions to Millicent about what to tell the police when they arrived. She gave her a T-shirt Kailey had worn yesterday in case they brought a dog. She found a recent photo.

And then she and Daniel were running, hand in hand, united by fear as love had not been able to unite them, to the edge of Copper.

They ran through the woods until they could run no more.

They came to a huckleberry patch.

'Kailey!' she shouted.

'Kailey!' Daniel cried.

Their voices echoed eerily back to them. The berries on the bushes were finished.

'There's a hundred huckleberry patches on this mountain,' Annie said.

'And Kailey's been to them all?' he deduced grimly.

'Yes.'

'She's a bright kid. She can find her way back out.'

But they both knew he had said it only to take the chill off the emptiness of the woods around them. Even adults got turned around in the dense woods. Even adults got hurt.

Suddenly the mountain seemed so big. The wilderness around them seemed so huge.

'Daniel, she's so small,' Annie whispered.

'We'll find her,' he said with determination.

But an awful fear had taken root in Annie—the fear that they wouldn't.

'There are bears up here, Daniel.'

'I know.'

'And cougars.'

'Hey,' he reminded her gently. 'You always said she made too much noise to get into that kind of trouble, and you were right.'

'She won't be making noise if she's scared and hungry. Or if she's hurt——' She could hear her voice rising wildly.

'Annie.' He took her face between his hands. 'Don't. Don't torture yourself. We're going to find her. I'm going to find her. I promise.'

Suddenly a promise from Daniel seemed like a solid thing, something one could hold on to when there was nothing left.

Why was that so? Why, when she knew that his promises were as shiny as bright pennies but made of wood?

But suddenly, looking into Daniel's eyes, she knew that she could trust this promise.

It came to her that she could trust Daniel. Completely. He would find Kailey.

'Do you want to go back to the house and see if she's turned up there yet, while I go further up the mountain?'

She shook her head. 'No. I want to be with you.' She left the forever unspoken.

He nodded, took her hand, and briefly squeezed it. Then, squaring his shoulders, he released her hand and went up the mountain slope.

Annie struggled to keep up with a stride made long and fast by sheer desperation. How far could a small child go? Would she have even come this way? Had she really come in search of berries, or had she gone somewhere else?

The whole town of Copper was ringed by formidable wilderness.

Thoughts like these plagued Annie, but Daniel's promise kept her going. She was hungry and tired, and a despair as heavy as death settled on her in the late afternoon, but she kept glancing at Daniel.

He would smile at her reassuringly and call again, though his voice was hoarse from calling. His enormous strength soothed her and held back the clouds of panic that threatened to overwhelm her.

They heard a helicopter pass over the mountain several times. The official search had begun.

Night began to fall.

'I don't want her alone in the dark up here,' Annie said, her voice an exhausted croak.

'Do you want to go check and see if she's back? If she's been found by someone else?'

He thought she was cracking. He thought it was getting to be too much for her. Because they could still hear the helicopter. Far away they could hear the tinny cry of bull-horns. He knew Kailey was not back, that she had not been found.

They came suddenly to a rocky outcropping that overlooked the town. The base of the mountain was alive with color. Searchlights and red and blue emergency-team lights lit up the sky. The forest flickered as though it was lit for Christmas with the small lights of hundreds of searchers going into it.

'They haven't found her,' Annie whispered. 'They haven't found my little girl. Dear God, don't let my little girl be dead.'

'She's not dead,' Daniel said fiercely. 'Let's go.'

She wanted to be worthy of him, and she called on reserves of strength and courage she had had no idea she possessed.

But the darkness shut in swiftly around them. Daniel plunged on desperately, but finally he was forced to stop, his breath ragged.

'We don't have lights,' he said. 'It's dark. We haven't eaten all day. You're cold.'

'Are you saying we have to quit?'

'I won't quit, Annie, but we're going to have to re-group. We'll need to eat. We need some basic supplies. If we find her we don't even have a candy bar to give her.'

'No,' Annie whispered. 'I can't go back down. It will take an hour. An hour that we could be looking, that we could find her.'

But even though she protested she registered how rational he was being—calm though the crisis had become more critical. No wonder her heart had never had a hope against him.

'Let's try one more thing before we go down, then. Sing,' Daniel commanded her softly. 'Sing, Annie.'

'What?'

'Your voice carries. She'd recognize that. Sing.'

The suggestion seemed utterly sane in a crazy way, and when she sang it felt so utterly right. The song came from deep within Annie. Deeper than it ever had before. It was a song that sang of life, that went up and down with joy and with sadness, that tumbled over the mountain air as naturally as water flowing over rocks. It was a song of strength and courage, pain and passion.

She closed her eyes and sang and sang. Her love-song.

To Kailey.

When she opened her eyes Daniel quickly turned his head. Not quickly enough that the moon didn't turn the single tear running down his cheek to silver.

Her admiration of his strength deepened. His heart was breaking and he had the courage to let that out, without being in any way diminished by it.

'Break's over,' he said gruffly. He held out his hand to her. She took it. 'We have to go back,' he told her gently.

'I know.' She knew that if Kailey was anywhere near here she would have heard the song. She listened to the night.

It did not sing sweetly back to her.

They went through the woods, staggering with hunger and exhaustion, but united for once.

What a terrible way to find out what a good team they made, Annie thought morosely. She should marry him if he would still have her.

It didn't matter if he loved her. It didn't matter if other women caught his eye from time to time. As long as he came back to her.

They were good together.

But it still mattered.

'Crazy Annie Calhoun,' she muttered to herself.

'Sorry, Annie, what did you say?' He tripped in the darkness and cursed softly.

Annie crumpled beside him.

'It won't be long now until we're down there,' he reassured her. He pulled her to her feet. She didn't want him to have to carry her but she could not help but lean heavily against him, feeling acutely the difference between a man and a woman. His stamina outstripped hers; he was stronger and more rugged. It made her feel protected and cared for in some primitive way. The blood of warriors and hunters still flowed strong in his veins. He would not rest until he had made his world right.

They passed a rescue-team coming up. Daniel showed them on a map where they had been. Annie looked at them—a man every few feet, flashlights scanning the ground. Their faces were grim and determined, but it was still the fire in Daniel's eyes that she looked to for reassurance.

It took them a precious hour to get back off the mountain. They staggered into the emergency camp and were given subdued greetings. Annie was overwhelmed by the number of people there.

Millicent, her face gray with exhaustion but her manner as militant as ever, came bustling over to them and guided them to a table set up in the glow of a lantern light.

'Sit,' she ordered.

They sat at a wooden table with folding chairs set up around it. The constant chatter of radios filled the air. They could see the lights bobbing up the mountain.

Annie laid her tired head on the table until Millicent put steaming bowls of soup and thick chunks of bread down in front of them. Scratchy blankets were thrown over their shoulders. She felt Daniel's hand come to rest on her shoulder as if it belonged there.

'There are volunteers here from a hundred miles away,' Millicent told her. 'Probably five hundred people are looking for Kailey.'

Annie nodded her gratitude. She ate her soup, her shoulders sagging with weariness. She watched as other searchers came in and more went out. Some, those who knew her even remotely, stopped and patted her on the shoulder, or said something reassuring.

'They love her,' she murmured. 'I can see it in their faces.'

'I've seen it in their faces all along,' Daniel said. 'How much they love both of you.'

She looked at him and held her breath for a moment, hoping he would say how much *he* loved both of them, but he said nothing else, eating his soup with appetite and urgency, his features grim and remote.

There was a great hollow feeling inside her as she gulped down the scalding hot coffee Millicent brought.

Daniel stood up. 'We need jackets and lights. Are you coming back with me?'

She nodded, grateful that he was willing to take her even though her sagging strength must be holding him back.

The hollow feeling inside her was for Kailey. She could not stand it if Daniel left her, too. Her misery would be too much to bear without him sharing it.

They went back up the mountain, warm and full, their way lit before them.

But Kailey was somewhere out there in the dark—cold, hungry and scared.

They had to find her soon.

'If I had agreed to marry you, would Kailey be gone right now?' she murmured, her overwrought mind beginning to wander in funny directions, exploring forbidden avenues.

Daniel whirled and looked at her. 'What did you say?'

'Nothing.'

'Annie, tell me what you said!'

'It was silly, but I wondered if she ran away when I spoiled her dream for her. She wanted you for her daddy more than anything else.'

Daniel was staring at her.

'What, Daniel?'

'I know where Kailey is,' he said with a weary smile. 'I think I know where Kailey is.'

She didn't know where he had got that final burst of energy from, but his reserves of strength astounded her again when he changed direction and began to jog.

'Daniel,' she called breathlessly. 'Please wait.'

He slowed, and held back his hand to her. She took it. It seemed as if a bright star shot through the heavens.

Soon she began to recognize where they were. He was taking them to the same place where they had gone for that picnic.

'Kailey!' he called, his voice nearly gone. 'Annie, sing.'

Her voice was nearly gone too, but she forced the tortured notes out of it.

'Shhh. Listen.'

Annie stopped singing. In the unearthly silence of the forest at night she heard the smallest sound.

She ran toward it.

Almost hidden under the low green branches of an alder bush was Kailey. She tugged Kailey out from under there, and pulled her sweet weight into the circle of her arms. Kailey felt limp. Her sobs were dry and nearly soundless.

Daniel dropped on his knees beside them, tore off his jacket and wrapped it around the shivering girl.

Kailey looked at him with tired eyes. Her eyes flicked to him, and to her mother, and back to him. She smiled thoughtfully.

Annie shifted her weight, and Daniel took Kailey from her. They sat shoulder to shoulder, joy, soundless, passing between them, leaping in the air all around them like angels dancing.

Kailey groaned. 'Don't touch my foot. Hurts.'

Her voice was a strained whisper. Annie realized she had probably called as often and as desperately as they.

'Know my way home,' Kailey whispered proudly, 'but I hurt my foot. Couldn't walk.' She shut her eyes.

Daniel shone his light on her foot and tenderly pulled back her sock. Her ankle was dark and bruised.

Her eyes opened, and she looked straight up at Daniel. She touched the stubble of his beard.

'It worked,' she breathed, 'just like you said it would.'

'You came to change your wish, didn't you?' he asked, his voice a hoarse rumble of emotion.

Slowly Kailey opened her fist. Inside her palm was a badly crushed flower.

A fairy-slipper.

'I didn't mean to pick the flower, but I got ever so scared and I wanted to be near it 'cause it was magic so I just sat beside it and held it but then it came off in my hand. Are you mad?'

'No, sweetheart. Nobody's mad.'

'I wasted that first wish,' she told them.

'Kailey, you don't have to tell us right now,' Annie said, not wanting her child to strain her voice any more.

'Haven't had anyone to talk to for ever so long,' Kailey came back swiftly.

Annie laughed with quiet pleasure. The night was soft around them. The look on Daniel's face right now would be etched tenderly on her mind forever. 'All right. You can talk if you want to.'

'I wasted my wish. The first time. I wished for a stupid kitty, but that's not what I really wanted.'

'What did you really want?' Annie asked, snuggling into the warmth of Daniel's shoulder, stroking her daughter's hair. She wished that this moment of perfect love for one another could last forever.

'A daddy, course. Then, when you and Daniel had that big fight last night, I knew it was my fault for wasting my wish on a dumb cat. I had to fix it. I just had to. And it worked, didn't it? You're my daddy now, aren't you?'

Annie felt Daniel's arms tighten around his daughter.

'Yeah,' he said gruffly. 'I'm your daddy now. And do you know what that means?'

'What?' Kailey asked with sleepy satisfaction. 'What does it mean, Daddy?'

'It means,' he said with aching tenderness, 'that I'll love you forever.' His eyes lifted from the top of Kailey's head and locked on Annie's.

Annie turned her head swiftly so that he would not see the emotion that gleamed suddenly in her eyes.

'And?' Kailey demanded.

'And what?' he asked, puzzled.

'Buy me presents on my birthday?'

'Yes, that too.'

'And ride me on your shoulders, course.'

'Course.'

'And——' her voice was fading away '—and come with me to the father and kid baseball game in Joo-ly.'

'Every July, forever and ever, as long as you want me there.'

Annie watched Kailey's eyes drift closed. The husky little voice was silent, and Kailey's breathing became deep and even.

'And,' Kailey's voice said suddenly, though the energy it took to reopen the eyes was apparently not available, 'marry up my mommy.'

Daniel didn't say anything.

Kailey started to snore.

The time had come, she thought, her weariness and her exhilaration combining to give her the courage to do what she needed to do.

'Daniel, if you asked me the question you asked me last night right now, you'd get a different answer.'

'I know,' he said softly. He seemed very sad.

'So, ask,' she suggested with soft pleading.

'No. Annie, it's all wrong. You're emotionally wrung-out. You're practically drunk with relief.'

Annie remembered the suitcases at his door... and Miranda.

She turned her head swiftly away from him again. How could history repeat itself with such brutal accuracy?

She had trusted him once before, and look where it had gotten her. And now she had trusted him again, with the same result.

He was absolutely right. She was drunk. Nearly out of her mind with exhaustion and relief and emotion. At least she hadn't completely humiliated herself by telling him how much she loved him.

'Annie——'

'Here she is!' a voice cried, and they were suddenly caught in the harsh beam of a strong light. 'We've found Kailey Calhoun!'

CHAPTER TEN

'GOODNIGHT, Daniel.' Goodbye my love. Annie was under her down comforter, Kailey, already sleeping, nestled in close beside her.

Annie's own eyes were so heavy that she didn't think she could keep them open one more second, and yet she was also having trouble closing them.

Daniel bent and kissed Kailey's cheek, and then hers.

'It's been a long, hard day. Go to sleep,' he said softly when she continued to look at him, taking this last chance to imprint his every feature on her mind.

His hair was still damp from a recent shower, the red highlights muted. It curled a bit where the tips touched the collar of his fresh shirt. The liveliness that usually lit his face from within was gone, and tired lines crinkled at the sides of his eyes. His eyes, usually leaping with life, were subdued with weariness.

She should let him go home. She closed her eyes and slipped with incredible swiftness into the abyss of sleep.

Daniel stood for a long time, watching. They looked like two Christmas card angels in high-necked white flannel nightgowns, with that black hair cascading around pink-flushed faces.

Annie's eyelashes were so long they cast shadows on her cheeks. Her lips were naturally full of colour, and parted slightly as she slept. If she had been awake, he might have taken it as an invitation to kiss her.

He was reluctant to leave them, though his own exhaustion was creeping through the muscles in his neck and lower back.

He should go home and sleep. There would be plenty
of time tomorrow to sort things through.

Kailey whimpered in her sleep and, shivering, tried to
burrow in closer to her mother.

He hesitated. Go home, he ordered himself. Instead,
he pulled back the corner of the quilt and slid into the
bed. He would just stay with them for a few minutes.
He had come so close to losing them both. He couldn't
bear to leave just yet. With Kailey in the middle, he
wrapped his arms around his two girls.

Kailey stopped shivering and whimpering. Annie gave
a sigh of such utter contentment that he smiled.

A deep feeling of peace came over him. Of gratitude.

He knew, with a sudden and startling clarity, that
things always turned out the way they were supposed to
be. He closed his eyes, just for a moment, to savor this
feeling of being so richly happy.

'Good morning, Mommy.'

'Good morning, honey,' Annie mumbled into her
pillow.

'Good morning, Daddy.'

Annie's eyes flew open. Cautiously she turned her
head. Daniel's head was on the pillow, not a full foot
away. Kailey was in between, looking infinitely pleased
with the arrangement. Annie squawked with startled
outrage.

Daniel's eyes opened, soft black, like velvet. His face
was dark with whiskers. For a moment he looked
puzzled, and then his eyes fastened on her face and he
smiled with drowsy pleasure.

'Mornin', Annie.' His voice had always been too sexy
for his own good, and it struck her as being even more
so in the very intimate confines of her bed.

'Mornin', Kailey.' He reached up and gave one of Kailey's tangled black curls a playful pull.

'What are you doing in my bed?' Annie asked, pulling the covers tight around her chin.

Daniel's eyes followed the movement with lazy amusement.

'He's my daddy, course,' Kailey told Annie with a displeased frown.

Daniel grinned devilishly at her.

Having resolved that to her satisfaction, Kailey got up and bounced down to the end of the bed and off.

'I'm going to make my mommy and daddy breakfast,' she announced. She came around to his side of the bed and peered at him. 'What would you like?'

'Bacon and eggs,' Daniel said. 'Toast, coffee, panca——'

Kailey gave him a thump on his arm. 'No, silly. Cornflakes or rice krispies?'

'Cornflakes,' he said solemnly.

'Rice krispies,' Annie said resignedly, watching Kailey march from the room. Now they were in the bed alone together.

'I thought you'd be long gone by now,' Annie told him tersely. She looked straight ahead. There was something infinitely wonderful about his weight in the bed next to her, about the way he looked in the morning, about his clean, masculine scent being in the air all around her.

'I'm not going anywhere.'

'You are so. I saw your suitcases.'

'I changed my mind.'

'Somehow that doesn't surprise me.' To her horror, her lip trembled. To her horror, he noticed, and reached up and placed an inquisitive finger on it.

'Why doesn't it surprise you?'

'Isn't that what you did, all those years ago?' she asked. She had wanted to sound uncaring. Instead her voice wobbled shamelessly.

'I'm not following you.'

'You said you'd love me forever,' she told him, her voice small and wounded. 'And then you changed your mind. You were gone.'

She didn't dare look at him. She examined the seam on her quilt instead.

'I have loved you forever,' he said softly.

She jerked her head and looked at him, searching his face for truth. Her heart was hammering in her throat, and it felt as if a million tears were building pressure behind the dam of her eyes.

It was in his eyes, if his eyes were to be believed.

'Me and all the other girls,' she said shakily.

'No, just you.'

'Come on, Daniel. I've seen the magic you work on women's unsuspecting hearts. Even the other night. You left here, and within minutes you were in a grope with Miranda.'

'That was not a grope!'

'Then what was it?'

'Annie, I'm not even sure. Every time I see that girl she looks like she's going to burst into tears, and the other night she did. She took one look at me and started bawling. I didn't know what to do. She looked so forlorn. So I gave her a quick hug. She let me hold her for a few seconds and then took off like a fox before the hounds.'

Suddenly it felt like too much work not to trust him.

If he said it was so, it was so. Her heart believed in him. She realized that her heart had never stopped believing in him.

'Annie,' he said softly, 'what happened between you and Jeff Turner all those years ago?'

'Between Jeff and I?' The question caught her off-balance, it seemed so unrelated to whether or not he loved her. 'What do you mean?'

'It was in September. Remember? I'd gotten a job bucking for a logging company. I had to be away at camp during the week, but I came home weekends. One weekend I came home and you were gone. With Jeff.'

She remembered every detail of that time in their lives. It was true. She had gone with Jeff. Reluctantly, because she hadn't wanted to miss her weekend with Daniel. But Jeff was a friend and he'd needed her. At the time she'd been so full of confidence. What was giving up one weekend when you had forever?

'Yes,' she said. 'I went with Jeff.'

She saw an iciness invade Daniel's features. 'Not like that, I didn't,' she gasped. 'His brother had been in a terrible accident in Alberta. He was too upset to drive, so I drove him. It was all in the note I left for you.'

'I never got a note from you, Annie.'

'But I left it right on your front porch. I even remember putting a rock on it so the wind wouldn't blow it away.'

'I got a message,' he said darkly. 'Not a note, a message.'

'What message?' she said with confusion.

'"Annie said to tell you that she's too young for forever."'

Annie felt the blood drain from her face.

'"Annie left town with Jeff Turner this morning, and it didn't look like they were planning on coming back for a long time."'

The pain hit Annie so hard that she stuffed her fist in her mouth and bit on it. 'Who would tell you that?' she whispered. 'Daniel, who would tell you such a terrible lie?'

'Miranda told me.'

'Miranda?' Annie whispered. 'Oh, no.'

Miranda had become her friend, and the treachery was almost too much to comprehend.

'Daniel, when I got back from Alberta Miranda phoned me from Vancouver. She said that she was with you, and that you were in love with her and you were going to get married. She said that neither of you had meant to hurt me, that it was something that had just happened.'

'What?' Daniel exploded. He yanked back the covers. There were white lines of anger around his mouth, and a muscle jerked spasmodically in the strong line of his jaw. His eyes had a killing light in them.

'I'm going to have a little talk with that girl,' he said, sitting on the edge of the bed and putting his shoes on. He was so angry that he snapped a lace in his runner. 'No wonder she cries every time she sees me. She knew that eventually I was going to find out. No wonder she's scared of me, and rightly so!'

'Wait, Daniel.'

'I can't. That witch stole six years of our lives from us. I'm going to go settle a very old score with her.' He got up, his anger a fearsome thing, crackling in the air around him.

'Daniel, calm down,' Annie ordered crisply.

He glared at her, but reluctantly perched on a corner of the bed.

She reached out and covered his hand with hers. 'Did you go to Vancouver with her?'

'Not the way it sounds. I was leaving. I'd waited until Sunday for you to come back, but you didn't. I just wanted to get away from here. I was so angry and hurt and confused. I just wanted to be going a hundred miles an hour down the road on my motorbike to anywhere where you weren't. Where memories of you weren't.

'Now that I think about it, Miranda was there quite a bit, listening to me rant and offering sympathy. I hardly noticed. Anyway, when I said that I was going she said she needed a lift to Vancouver, and that seemed as good a place as any.'

'But nothing happened between you?'

'Annie, what do you take me for? I was in love with you.' Suddenly his eyes darkened. 'So that's what you've taken me for all these years. Well, for your information, I dropped Miranda off at her aunt's, or something, and never saw her again until I came back here. A hundred miles an hour down the highway hadn't done it, so I figured maybe a million miles between us would. I signed on as a deck-hand on a ship bound for China because I wanted to get as far away from you as I could.

'But the truth was that I couldn't outrun my own misery. I couldn't stand China because you weren't there with me. The one I laughed with, and cried with, and shared my soul with wasn't there.

'The truth is that I tried for six years to get you out of my system, and I never could. I never stopped loving you, Annie. I remembered telling you that summer that I would love you forever, and sometimes I would think of those words and think I had doomed myself to be alone forever.'

'Oh, Daniel,' she whispered.

'Annie, how could I ever stop loving you?'

She was in his arms. 'I never stopped loving you, either, Daniel.' She lifted her head and gave him a watery smile. 'When you came back I tried so hard not to let it show. I feel all these things for you that scare me to death. I thought you'd betrayed me once, and that I shouldn't be feeling all the same things again. That I should be older and wiser——'

'Things?' he teased, his hand lightly tracing the full curve of her breast.

'It scared me because I thought I was going to be like my mother—destined forever to love men incapable of loving me back. Destined forever to be a victim of my own uncontrollable passion. I couldn't have that kind of life for Kailey.'

Daniel threw back his head and laughed.

'It's not funny, worrying if you've inherited hormones gone wild.'

Daniel laughed harder.

'You stop it!'

'Annie, I'm sorry,' he choked, 'but I just can't believe what you're saying.'

'I am very passionate.'

'I know that,' he told her softly. 'You're red-hot. But, Annie, you've been faithful to the same man for six years and he wasn't even with you. Can you think of anything more different from your mother?'

It came to her slowly, that languid feeling of freedom. The freedom of being a one-man woman. The wondrous feeling of knowing Daniel was right.

She was not her mother. She had broken the cycle.

'You know, Daniel, it wasn't just physical anyway. I mean, I tried to tell myself that, but being so drawn to you was more than physical.'

'I know.'

'Some people search all their lives for a soulmate, but I found mine the summer I turned eighteen. My heart would never let me forget. My heart recognized the truth, even though my head tried to overrule it.'

'It's an easy head to forgive,' Daniel said, placing a kiss on the tip of her nose.

'I think we have some other forgiving to do,' she said softly.

'I'll never forgive her. Never.'

'Daniel, why would she do something so awful?' Annie asked him gently.

'I don't know,' he said angrily.

'I do,' she said tenderly. Yes, she knew all too well what the pain of loving someone who you thought didn't love you back did to a person's spirit. Twisted it, somehow. 'In time, she'll tell us. Let's trust her to do the right thing.'

'Sure,' Daniel snorted.

'Maybe that's even why she came here yesterday?'

'She did come here yesterday, didn't she?' he said slowly. 'I'd kind of forgotten about that.'

'Remember how she reacted at that meeting, when we were kind of squabbling?'

'Yeah,' he said reluctantly. 'I do.'

'I think she felt responsible for the fact that we weren't getting along.'

'Well, she was!'

Annie gave him a look.

'Indirectly,' he conceded gruffly.

'I think, Daniel, that if you give love a chance, it will look after everything. Heal everything.'

'I have a hurt right here that needs healing,' he said, placing a hand dramatically over his heart.

'Let me show you,' she whispered, dropping her head to his hand and kissing it. She shoved it gently out of her way, opened his shirt, and kissed his heated skin, right above his heart.

'It hurts here, too,' he teased, touching a finger to his lips.

Wantonly, she coiled her arms around his neck, and pulled his lips down to her own.

'Now, that's precisely what a mommy and daddy are supposed to do,' a pleased voice informed them. 'Smooching.'

'Kailey?'

'Yes, Daddy?'

'Breakfast is going to be delayed.'

'That's okay. I can't pour the milk, and the rice krispies accidentally went on the floor.'

'Now that Daddy is here,' Annie said, 'we have to have a new rule.'

'What?' Kailey asked suspiciously. 'I don't much like rules.'

'When our bedroom door is shut, you are not allowed in here.'

'That's not a hard rule,' Kailey said with a shrug. 'Cartoons are on now. Can I watch them?'

'By all means,' Daniel said thickly.

'And can I have cookies and ice-cream for breakfast?' Kailey asked.

'No!' Annie said, with hardly any firmness at all.

'Just this once,' Daniel said huskily, 'you can have whatever you want for breakfast.'

'Oh, goody!'

'And shut the door behind you.'

*   *   *

'Annie, I think we should get some alpacas.'

'Alpacas?' She looked tenderly down at the man who was stretched out on her coach, his head in her lap.

'I want to stay here, in Copper. I can do most of the administration for Wild Melody from anywhere. My store managers are excellent. And I was thinking that I could expand my business and offer guided hikes and trekking in the summer, cross-country ski trips in the winter.'

'There are no alpacas in Canada!' she told him.

'You're wrong, Annie. There are. Llamas and alpacas are becoming big business here. They make ideal animals and the wool is very profitable.'

'I've been wrong before,' she told him. She had been. She had wasted precious time listening to her head instead of her heart. Now she loved these quiet times in the evening, together with Daniel after Kailey had gone to bed.

'I could promote trips through the stores.'

'It would be wonderful if we could stay in Copper.'

'But you'd move with me if we had to?'

She knew, then, that the issues of her childhood were finally resolved. She didn't feel a need to stay in one place to give Kailey that feeling of stability she had never had. It hadn't ever been about staying in one place—it had been about staying with one person.

'I'd follow you to the ends of the earth if you asked me to, and you know it.'

He smiled at her. 'I've been meaning to ask you something.'

'Yes?'

'In fact, I've been ordered by Millicent to ask you——'

The doorbell rang.

He unfolded himself from the couch. 'Saved by the bell.'

He opened the door. Annie could see Miranda there, and she glanced uncertainly at Daniel, not sure of the reception he would give her.

His face, as he opened the door and stood back from it, was not exactly friendly.

'Hello, Miranda,' Daniel said. Annie noticed that his voice was perfectly civil.

Daniel gave her the smile of a man too satisfied to be angry.

'I need to talk to you both,' Miranda said nervously. She perched on the edge of a chair and looked down at her hands. She knotted them and unknotted them.

She cleared her throat. 'I did something terrible,' she whispered. 'I came to ask you to forgive me.'

She looked at her hands for a long time. Tears dripped down her face. She took a deep breath. 'Daniel, when we were teenagers I fell in love with you.'

'What?' Daniel exclaimed. 'Miranda, you didn't even like me. I remember——'

Annie squeezed his hand and he fell silent.

Miranda's eyes skittered around the room. 'I know I seemed not to like you. I was kind of scared of how much I liked you, afraid you wouldn't like me back, so I was always saying those awful things. I was so sacred around you that I always ended up acting so dumb.'

'Miranda,' he said softly. 'I never meant to scare you. I've never scared anyone.'

'It wasn't you,' Miranda said, 'it was me. I can see that now. But back then I was just a mixed-up kid who wanted you so badly and didn't know what to do about it.'

'I'm sorry,' Daniel said. 'I never knew.'

'How could you know?' Miranda said, and smiled shakily at him, looking him in the eyes for the first time. 'When Annie came along and things started to happen between you I was beside myself with jealousy. Watching Annie, I realized I had gone about getting you to notice me all the wrong way, and I thought that if I just had another chance...'

She was looking at them both now, her gaze as clear and steady as Annie had ever seen it.

'One day I went over to see you, I was going to pretend I needed a ride to Nelson or something, and I saw Annie leaving something on your front step. I went up there after and saw the letter, and I took it. It was like I couldn't help myself. I took it and I read it. Annie had gone away with Jeff because his brother had been hurt. I saw it as an opportunity. It was like from the moment I made the decision to take that letter, there was no going back. I just kept getting in deeper and deeper, becoming more and more committed to doing something wrong in the stupid hope that I could make things right for me.

'I told you Annie didn't love you. I made it sound like there was more to her going away with Jeff than there was. And then I hung around, trying to get you to notice me, but you were too upset.

'I hitched that ride with you to Vancouver thinking it would change. That eventually you might turn to me for comfort, that you might fall in love with me, finally. I even phoned Annie and told her you were in love with me, that we would probably get married. It was my greatest fantasy. But you dropped me off at my aunt's, and I waited and waited for you to call, but you didn't. Then I ran into somebody else from Copper who had seen you, and they said you had gone to China.'

A silence filled the room and swam around them.

'I came back here. I hadn't known Annie was pregnant. I'm ashamed to say I don't know if it would have changed all the things I did. I tried to make it up to her. I worked in her shop, and worked for the town, but nothing ever seemed to make the lump of guilt inside me go away. Nothing except this.'

She looked relieved. She was still looking directly at them. Her hands were folded in her lap. Her shoulders were back.

'A little while ago,' she finished, 'I met a man in Trail. I realized I could never hope to be happy with him as long as this was hanging over my head.

'I'm sorry. I hurt so many people. It was a stupid, self-centered, sick thing to do. If both of you decide never to speak to me again, I'll understand.'

'Miranda,' Daniel said gently, 'will you forgive me for being so young and full of myself as not to notice that someone cared about me?'

Miranda's eyes clouded with tears. 'Thank you, Daniel,' she whispered.

Annie had never felt so proud of the man she loved.

'Miranda,' she said softly, 'I think I'm going to need some help with a kind of big project. Can I count on you?'

Miranda nodded again, the tears spilling down her eyes. 'How could I do that to you two? It's so obvious that you belong together.'

'When things are meant to be,' Daniel said softly, 'they always find a way.'

After Miranda had left he looked at Annie mischievously. 'What big project is that?' he asked.

'Oh, pop the question, Daniel, before Millicent comes over here with her shotgun.'

*　　*　　*

Soft autumn sunshine spilled through the stained glass of the small church. The building was overflowing with late-blooming fall flowers.

The twelve pews were packed to overflowing. The wedding march began.

A broad-shouldered man stood at the altar, waiting, his black eyes trained on the back door of the church. He was dressed in a long-tailed white tuxedo, his hands folded calmly in front of him.

The back door burst open and a small girl danced in, her white dress floating around her, a crown of flowers caught in her black curls. She carried a wicker basket with a pillow and a ring.

'That's my daddy,' she informed several onlookers as she made her way down the aisle, hippety-hopping. She remembered, stopped, and began again, walking with grave dignity for a few steps until the bounce took over once more.

'Beautiful job on the dress, Miranda,' someone whispered.

'Hi, Daddy,' Kailey said, arriving at the altar. She looked at him with awe. 'You look just like a prince in a storybook.'

'A white knight,' he corrected her quietly. He smiled at her, and then his eyes returned to the door.

It opened again. Millicent marched in, lovely in pale peach silk.

'Miranda, did you make that dress, too?' someone whispered.

Daniel smiled as Millicent joined them at the altar.

'Hi, Millie,' Kailey crowed.

Millicent gave her a stern look of warning.

The back door of the church opened again.

Annie entered, her dress, white Indian cotton, calf-length, the full skirt embroidered with lace, sweeping around her, the soft sleeves puffing around her arms, her smooth shoulders naked and lovely.

'Miranda,' a tearful voice whispered, 'I have never seen such a beautiful dress.'

Annie came down the aisle. She looked like a vision—like a young maiden who danced in the forest to an untamed melody of her own.

'Ooooh,' Kailey breathed. 'Doesn't she look ever so bee-yoo-ti-ful?'

'Yes,' Daniel breathed.

Millicent gave Kailey an evil look.

Annie smiled greetings at her friends and her neighbors, but her eyes returned again and again to the man who waited for her at the altar.

Her eyes were glowing with the soft light of a woman so certain in the love she both gave and received.

She arrived at the altar and took her place beside Daniel. For a long time in the hush of the church they stood drinking in each other with loving eyes.

'Who gives this woman?' the minister asked.

'I do,' Millicent said, that stern old voice softened.

'Dearly beloved, we are gathered——'

A funny look came across the minister's face. He stepped back and gave his vestments a firm shake that did nothing to dislodge the kitten clawing its way up him.

Daniel stepped forward quickly and disentangled the kitten, white with two shockingly black eyes, from the minister's frock. He stood looking helplessly at the intruder until Brook came forward and shyly offered to look after it until the ceremony was over.

Daniel handed over the kitten and looked sternly at Kailey, but his lips were twitching and it was evident that he was trying very hard not to join the howls of laughter behind him.

'That's my kitten,' Kailey informed the minister angelically. 'He wanted to come ever so badly, so I put him in my basket under the pillow. I guess he couldn't see.'

The laughter had died by the time she said her next words, and they fell, clear and crystal, into the sacred silence of the church.

'His name is Love.'

'His name is Love,' the minister repeated slowly.

A hush fell over those gathered, a hush that sang with the untamed melody of those words, with the holiness of them.

'Dearly beloved,' the minister began again as Annie's hand crept into the welcoming warmth of Daniel's, 'we are gathered here today to celebrate the miracle of Love.'

'Amen,' Kailey said vehemently.

MILLS & BOON

are proud to present...

A set of warm, involving romances in which you can meet some fascinating members of our heroes' and heroines' families. Published each month in the Romance series.

Look out for "Simply the Best" by Catherine Spencer in July 1995.

Family Ties: Romances that take the family to heart.

MILLS & BOON

Kids & Kisses—where kids and romance go hand in hand.

This summer Mills & Boon brings you Kids & Kisses— a set of titles featuring lovable kids as the stars of the show!

**Look out for
Love Without Measure by Caroline Anderson
in July 1995 (Love on Call series).**

Kids…one of life's joys, one of life's treasures.

Kisses…of warmth, kisses of passion, kisses from mothers and kisses from lovers.

In Kids & Kisses…every story has it all.

Available from W.H. Smith, John Menzies, Volume One, Forbuoys, Martins, Woolworths, Tesco, Asda, Safeway and other paperback stockists.

SPRING FLOWER COMPETITION

How would you like a years supply of Temptation books ABSOLUTELY FREE? Well, you can win them all! All you have to do is complete the word puzzle below and send it in to us by 31st December 1995. The first 5 correct entries picked out of the bag after that date will win a years supply of Temptation books (*four books every month - worth over £90*). What could be easier?

COWSLIP

BLUEBELL

PRIMROSE

DAFFODIL

ANEMONE

DAISY

GORSE

TULIP

HONESTY

THRIFT

L	L	E	B	E	U	L	B	Q
P	R	I	M	R	O	S	E	A
I	D	O	D	Y	U	I	P	R
L	O	X	G	O	R	S	E	Y
S	T	H	R	I	F	T	M	S
W	P	I	L	U	T	F	K	I
O	E	N	O	M	E	N	A	A
C	H	O	N	E	S	T	Y	D

PLEASE TURN OVER FOR DETAILS OF HOW TO ENTER

HOW TO ENTER

Hidden in the grid are various British flowers that bloom in the Spring. You'll find the list next to the word puzzle overleaf and they can be read backwards, forwards, up, down, or diagonally. When you find a word, circle it or put a line through it.

After you have completed your word search, don't forget to fill in your name and address in the space provided and pop this page in an envelope (you don't need a stamp) and post it today. Hurry - competition ends 31st December 1995.

Mills & Boon Spring Flower Competition,
FREEPOST,
P.O. Box 344,
Croydon,
Surrey. CR9 9EL

Are you a Reader Service Subscriber?   Yes ❏   No ❏

Ms/Mrs/Miss/Mr _____

Address _____

_____

_____ Postcode _____

One application per household.   **F**

You may be mailed with other offers from other reputable companies as a result of this application. If you would prefer not to receive such offers, please tick box. ❏

COMP395